BENNY BENSKY

AND THE PARROT-NAPPER

BENNY BENSKY
AND THE PARROT-NAPPER

by Mary Borsky

Illustrations by Linda Hendry

Tundra Books

Text copyright © 2008 by Mary Borsky
Illustrations copyright © 2008 by Linda Hendry

Published in Canada by Tundra Books,
75 Sherbourne Street, Toronto, Ontario M5A 2P9

Published in the United States by Tundra Books of Northern New York,
P.O. Box 1030, Plattsburgh, New York 12901

Library of Congress Control Number: 2007938846

Library and Archives Canada Cataloguing in Publication

    Benny Bensky and the parrot-napper/ Mary Borsky ; illustrations by
Linda Hendry.

Ages 8 to 11.
ISBN 978-0-88776-840-8

    I. Hendry, Linda   II. Title.

PS8553.O735B458 2008   jC813'.54   C2007-906212-1

We acknowledge the financial support of the Government of Canada
through the Book Publishing Industry Development Program (BPIDP)
and that of the Government of Ontario through the Ontario Media
Development Corporation's Ontario Book Initiative. We further
acknowledge the support of the Canada Council for the Arts and the
Ontario Arts Council for our publishing program.

ONTARIO ARTS COUNCIL
CONSEIL DES ARTS DE L'ONTARIO

Design by Kelly Hill
Typeset in Caslon

Printed in Canada

1 2 3 4 5 6   13 12 11 10 09 08

For Tenille and Carter
– M.B.

For Les and the girls
– L.H.

ACKNOWLEDGMENTS

For editorial assistance, I wish to thank Lauren Bailey, Julia Campbell, and Kathy Lowinger.

– M.B.

CONTENTS

1	A Zillion Candy Wrappers	1
2	Guess What?	9
3	A Dime a Dozen	24
4	Suspect Number One	34
5	So Long, Peanut	44
6	Plastic Hot Dog	55
7	Dog-Gone!	62
8	Parrots and Pirates	78
9	Just Leave Me Alone!	93
10	The Play's the Thing!	100
11	What a Dog! What a Detective!	110

A Zillion Candy Wrappers

The sky was blue, the grass was green, and the sun was bright as a zillion candy wrappers. Benny Bensky braced his furry black feet on the ground and flung his large doggie self after the Frisbee. His doggie grin cut through the morning air, his black ears flapped in the breeze, his long tail steered like a rudder. With a bite of his strong white teeth, Benny caught the Frisbee – *SNAP!* – just like that!

As he wagged his tail at his human companions, Benny Bensky heard someone calling from across the field.

"Yooo-hooo!" It was a cheery but commanding voice, and it carried nicely in the morning air.

Benny's furry black forehead scrunched up over his brown tadpole-shaped eyebrows. He looked about him, the edge of the red Frisbee still clamped in his mouth.

His owner, ten-year-old Rosie (who'd thrown the Frisbee), was on his left. Rosie's best friend, Fran (whose arms were already up in the air, ready for the next catch), was on his right. Just beyond, he could see a mother helping her little boy toss bread to the ducks in the river. He could see a curly-haired, teenaged boy with a carrier bag slung across his shoulder. There were two girls on a bicycle built for two: one with pink hair, the other with green hair.

"Is someone calling *us*?" asked Rosie, pushing her glasses up her lightly freckled nose.

"Ro-sie! Fra-an!" the high musical voice called again, a little closer this time.

"Who's that?" asked Fran, as she slipped a scrunchie from her wrist and pulled her long black hair into a ponytail.

The three friends stared across the green grass to see a plump, silver-haired woman climb out of a taxicab on the road at the edge of the park. The silver-haired woman turned and began to run toward them. As she ran, her hands flapped frantically this way and that, reminding Benny of windshield wipers on a rainy day.

"Why, it's *Mrs. Graham,*" said Rosie, her blue eyes round with surprise. "You know. She lives in that big brick house right next to the community center."

"Thank goodness I've found you!" Mrs. Graham said breathlessly, as she arrived in the middle of the field, where Benny, Rosie, and Fran were standing. Mrs. Graham stopped to catch her breath, pressing one hand on the string of pearls that looped down her heaving flowery chest. "I need a *huge* favor, girls. Please, please, *please* don't say no!" She gazed pleadingly at them from behind her wire-rimmed spectacles. "You see, I need someone to baby-sit my dear parrot, Peanut, for a few days. My daughter, Anna, is having twins – *twins!* – and I'm off this minute to the train station. I'll be back on Sunday!" She looked at her wristwatch and added, "Good gracious! I can't be late!"

Hastily, Mrs. Graham leaned forward to kiss Rosie and Fran in the middle of their foreheads, then a somewhat startled Benny, whom she kissed

– *SMACK!* – between his ears. She pressed a brass key into Rosie's hand. "Oh, and kids, have fun! Peanut's a barrel of laughs, you'll see. He's Mr. Personality Plus! He absolutely *thrives* on attention." She glanced at her watch again and then turned to run back across the grassy field, her flowery dress flapping in the breeze, her large handbag thumping at her side.

The three friends watched wordlessly while Mrs. Graham climbed into the backseat of the waiting taxi. She waved from the moving window, blew another kiss, and called, "I'm going to be a grand-mother! A grandmother of twins!"

Rosie, Fran, and Benny stared in the direction the taxicab had gone, then looked down at the shiny key in Rosie's hand.

"Parrot-sitting?" said Rosie with a slowly growing smile. Her curly hair shone in a coppery halo around her face. "That sounds like fun, doesn't it, Fran? I know all about pet-sitting. I baby-sat a gecko once."

"I baby-sat a Siamese fighting fish," Fran added. The three friends strolled homeward, Benny in the middle. "It was cinchy."

As they approached the entrance of the park, they passed the curly-haired, teenaged boy they'd seen earlier.

"Parrot-sitting?" he said with a grin. "Boy-oh-boy! I bet you have no clue what you got yourselves into." Rosie, Fran, and Benny stopped walking and looked at the boy in surprise. He had pale skin, dark shoulder-length curls, and a roll of tape was in one of his hands. "Parrots are picky eaters, you know! And that's just for starters!"

The three friends only stared (for they knew it was not a good idea to talk to strangers), but the curly-haired, teenaged boy did not seem to mind and cheerfully continued chatting. "Parrots need to be talked to, they need to be held, they need to be played with, they need to be cleaned up after, they need to be fed, they need to be kept out of drafts, and I-don't-know-what-all! Plus, I bet you don't know there's a parrot-napping ring in town, do you?"

Benny's ears pricked up; he looked toward Rosie, then Fran.

"We're not allowed to talk to strangers," Fran informed him. Both Rosie and Fran took a step backward. Rosie bent down to hold Benny by his collar, and Benny, taking this as his cue, growled in a mildly menacing way.

The boy ignored Benny. He scratched his skinny arm, blew a large pink bubble, and waited until it popped before he pulled a poster from his bag and taped it to a telephone pole.

"See this? We're advertising my band, The Pirates. We're playing tomorrow night!" The boy pointed proudly to the poster he'd just taped up.

From where they stood, Rosie, Fran, and Benny studied the poster, which read as follows:

THE PIRATES
HEAR THEM AT THE LAIR
8 P.M. FRIDAY
Be There or Be Square!

Benny looked up at the skull-and-crossbones design on the front of the boy's black T-shirt.

"Yup," the curly-haired boy added. "I'm the drummer." He tucked his tape dispenser under his arm, pulled two more rolled-up posters from his carrier bag, then drummed the air with the posters, meanwhile providing his own sound effects. "Ta-ta-ta-*too*, ta-ta-ta-*too*, ta-ta-ta-ta ta-ta-*too*."

Then he went back to taping up posters, this time to the side of a garbage can. "*Parrot-nappers*," he called to them over his shoulder. "Get it? You know, like *kidnappers*. Only parrot-nappers kidnap parrots. In fact – *as we speak*! – parrot-nappers are probably parrot-napping more parrots right here in our town of Smith Falls!"

Rosie and Fran's eyes grew very wide and, again, they looked at each other. They moved close to Benny.

"Darn!" the boy said. He whirled the empty roll on his tape dispenser. "Out of tape!" Benny could see that only one side of the poster about The Pirates was fastened to the garbage can.

The curly-haired boy pulled the pink bubble gum from his mouth and divided it into two sticky pieces. He stuck one piece of bubble gum under each of the loose corners of the poster and, while Benny watched with admiration, the boy pressed the poster to the garbage can.

"Why so glum, chums?" the boy asked, standing up and tossing his dark curls over the shoulder of his black skull-and-crossbones T-shirt. "You might be lucky. The parrot-nappers might get every other parrot in Smith Falls, but they still might not get *your* parrot. Look on the bright side! It might not happen to you."

Guess What?

"**M**ummy! Daddy!" shrieked Rosie. Rosie and Fran and Benny were out of breath by the time they got back to Rosie and Benny's house. "Guess what! You'll never guess what happened!"

Rosie's mother, Mrs. Bensky, curtsied to the children as they tumbled in through the door. She was dressed in a glittery gown, and she had a gold crown on her head.

"Hello my small but precious subjects," she smiled.

Benny, Rosie, and Fran stood still, their eyes wide.

"Our costumes just arrived," explained Mrs. Bensky, spreading out the shimmery skirt of her gown. "Remember I told you about the Smith Falls Theater Festival? Remember how your dad and I auditioned for parts in a play? Well, Mr. Bellefleur picked *us*! We're in *Hamlet*!"

"I have the lead role!" Mr. Bensky, Rosie's father, announced proudly. He was wearing black tights and was sword-fighting with an egg flipper in the hallway to the kitchen. "I'm the prince of Denmark! I *look* like the prince of Denmark, don't I?"

Rosie, Fran, and Benny stared at the egg flipper and at Mr. Bensky's tights.

"Umm . . ." said Rosie.

"Well . . ." said Fran.

"And I'm his mother, the queen," said Mrs. Bensky, swirling around in a fiery pirouette. "Did Mrs. Graham find you, by the way? She came here looking for you, Rosie."

"Mrs. Graham wants us to parrot-sit her parrot, Mrs. Bensky," explained Fran. "Her daughter is having twins and . . ."

". . . Twins?" exclaimed Mrs. Bensky, clapping her hands together. "Oh, my! Now, isn't that splendid!

Twins! What a surprise! And you're caring for her parrot! I'm so proud of you girls! How *neighborly* of you to help her out! Oh, by the way, girls, our director, Mr. Bellefleur, dropped off costumes for you. Rosie and Fran, you're in the play too! Isn't that exciting?" Mrs. Bensky held up two white dresses with puffy sleeves and long flouncy skirts.

"Me and Fran?" said Rosie, her mouth dropping open, her glasses sliding down her nose. "In the play? But we didn't even audition!"

"You don't have to learn lines," explained Mr. Bensky. "You just scatter flowers."

"But, Mummy! Daddy!" protested Rosie.

"It's already been decided," Mrs. Bensky said firmly. "Mr. Bellefleur wants you both to be the flower girls. You'll scatter white Kleenex flowers in the scenes where someone dies."

"Or gets murdered," explained Mr. Bensky cheerfully. "Which happens quite a lot in this play!"

"We *can't*!" said Rosie. "We're too busy *parrotsitting*! Anyway, I don't want to wear a dress!"

"But these dresses are *pretty*!" said Fran, holding one of the white dresses up to herself. "Come on, Rosie!" She pulled the long white dress over her

T-shirt and shorts and stood in front of the hallway mirror, swishing her long black hair as she whirled about. "Come on, Rosie! It'll be fun!"

"Mr. Bellefleur is big on *mood*," explained Mr. Bensky. "Like, when it's sad, boy-oh-boy, it better be *really* sad!"

"We can't let Mr. Bellefleur down," said Mrs. Bensky. "He puts so much into it. He wants the play to be something no one in Smith Falls will ever forget."

"Come *on*, Rosie!" Fran turned to Rosie who was sitting at the bottom of the stairs with her arms crossed. "Let's do it! It'll be *fun*! We can parrot-sit Mrs. Graham's parrot *and* be in the play!" Fran dropped the second dress over Rosie's head and helped her pull it on. Fran pressed her palms together. "Pretty pretty *pret-ty* please, Rosie?"

Rosie looked down doubtfully at the snowy-white dress.

"I'll be your friend forever and ever, Rosie! *Pleeeease?*"

"Okay," said Rosie, "I guess." She turned to her parents. "Mummy? Daddy? About the parrot? Mrs. Graham's parrot that we're parrot-sitting? You know what else we found out? . . ."

". . . You better be extra careful with that parrot, kids," Mr. Bensky said, out of breath from his sword-fighting and leading everyone into the kitchen. "There's a parrot-napping ring operating here in Smith Falls. Heard it on the radio a half an hour ago. Don't want them to get their hands on Mrs. Graham's bird." He pulled open the fridge and stuck his head inside for a better look. "Now, where the heck is that smoked salmon? I know it's here. Top shelf to the right. I'm sure that's where I put it."

"Oh, Daddy!" said Rosie, fingers to her lips. She looked up at him over her glasses. "Sor-*ry*! You see, Daddy, well, smoked salmon's Benny's favorite!"

"But . . . but . . ." yelped Mr. Bensky, "smoked salmon's *my* favorite too!"

Benny wagged his tail and bunted Mr. Bensky affectionately with his nose.

"Anna with twins!" laughed Mrs. Bensky. She bent down to hug Rosie. "Why, Rosie, do you remember? Anna Graham used to be *your* baby-sitter when *you* were just a tiny baby!"

"This dress is so pretty!" laughed Fran, twirling about in the kitchen to see the ruffled white skirt circle out around her. "Isn't it pretty, Mrs. Bensky?

Wait 'till I tell my mum! She'll take one hundred pictures! Rosie and I are in the play, too!"

"I'm not scared of any dumb old parrot-napper," announced Rosie as the three friends made their way to Mrs. Graham's house. She cleared her throat, looked around her, then spoke more boldly. "I'm not scared an inchy-pinchy bit!" She pushed her glasses up and pushed her curly red hair behind her ears, her voice a little quieter. "Are *you* scared, Fran?"

"Not a speck!" declared Fran. "If the parrot-napper steals Mrs. Graham's parrot, we'll just solve the mystery and get the parrot back again!"

Exactly! thought Benny, who grinned widely in happy agreement.

"We've solved mysteries before," Rosie pointed out, bending down to stroke Benny's silky black ears. "Plus, we have a big, fierce, black dog to protect us. Benny's great protection from a parrot-napper, don't you think, Fran?"

"Absolutely!" answered Fran. "One look at a big, black dog like Benny, and the parrot-napper is going to run the other way!"

Benny bounded up Mrs. Graham's front steps. He banged his tail on her metal porch railing. *Bling!*

Bling! Bling! Then he turned toward the street and barked boldly.

I'm a match for any parrot-napper! Benny announced to the world at large, continuing his barking. *My doggie brain is in top working order! My eyes are sharp and bright! My amazing doggie nose is picking up dozens of tantalizing smells! Garbage from the bins in front of the community center next door, the smell of a cat — make that two cats! The rubbery smell of Rosie's brand-new runners, the smell of the peanut-butter cookie in Fran's pocket, and . . . wait, what's that other delicious smell?*

Benny stopped barking for a moment while he lifted his large black nose into the air. He inhaled again, then bounded back to the sidewalk to snap up a cookie some baby had dropped from its stroller. The cookie was arrowroot and only slightly chewed around the edges. *Mmmm! Dee-licious!*

Rosie pulled the brass key out of her pocket and was about to fit it into the lock when she looked toward the house on the other side of Mrs. Graham's.

"Fran?" she said. "See that man on the porch next door? That's Mr. Bellefleur. He's the director of the play my mum and dad are in. Mummy and Daddy say he always wears that red cape and purple beret."

"I can tell he's a real artist," said Fran in a respect-ful whisper. "That's why he wants us to wear white dresses and scatter white Kleenex flowers at all the sad parts."

"Yeah," said Rosie, scratching a mosquito bite on her bare leg. "I guess."

Benny looked across to the neighboring yard to see a man with a purple beret and a fiery red cloak pacing back and forth on the front porch, talking to himself and flinging his hands about in the air.

"Does he always talk to himself that way?" Fran asked. "What's he saying?"

Benny, Rosie, and Fran strained their ears to listen.

"It sounds like he's saying, 'The birds, the birds, the birds,'" said Fran. "But, why's he saying that? There's not a bird in the sky."

"Oh, I know," Rosie said. "There's another play in the theater festival called *The Birds*, and he's directing that one, too."

"I wonder if *that* one has flower girls?" asked Fran, looking hopefully over to Mr. Bellefleur.

"*No*. It doesn't," said Rosie, turning the brass key in Mrs. Graham's front door. "I'm positive it doesn't have flower girls."

The oak door swung open.

From somewhere inside Mrs. Graham's house, a telephone began to ring. *Brrrrring! Brrrrring!*

Benny, Rosie, and Fran stepped onto the thick carpet in the hallway and shut the door behind them. Benny raised his large black nose into the air. The house smelled of lemon oil, polished wood, and some flowery smell, possibly lilacs.

Brrrrring! Brrrrring!

"Where's the phone?" whispered Fran. "Are we supposed to answer it?"

Rosie raised her hands, palms up, in the air and shrugged.

Cautiously and quietly, Benny, Rosie, and Fran made their way across the carpeted hallway and over the polished kitchen floor.

Without warning, Benny felt his four feet skid out in four different directions from under him and he landed – *SMACK!* – on his belly. Rosie grabbed his collar and helped him stand up again. Benny grinned sheepishly. Mrs. Graham's tiled kitchen floor was as slippery as a skating rink!

Brrrrring! Brrrrring!

The three comrades followed the ringing sound to the sunroom at the back of the house. Once there, Benny looked about him in bewilderment. The sunroom contained a pale-green couch, a bamboo rocker, a glass-topped coffee table, and a large tropical plant.

Brrrrring! Brrrrring!

Where was the phone? Benny sat down and scratched his head. He looked underneath the coffee table, then behind the couch. Then Benny noticed a tall brass cage tucked away underneath the fronds of the large tropical plant.

Inside the shadowy cage, on a rope slung from one side to the other, sat a bundle of dusty gray feathers shaped like a bird. The bird's head was gray, its wings were gray, its back was gray, and its tail was gray. Its curved beak and wizened clawed feet were gray. Its one visible eye was gray. *No big surprise here,* Benny noted.

Then the gray eye blinked.

Benny's eyes widened. His ears stood up in surprise.

Why! This must be the parrot, Benny thought. *Peanut the Parrot. And what a pathetic gray creature Peanut is. Aren't parrots supposed to come in bright colors? Aren't parrots supposed to be full of chatter and jokes and lively tricks? This parrot has clearly been shortchanged! This parrot has as much personality as a dirty feather duster in the back of a cleaning cupboard!*

Benny couldn't imagine any parrot-napper wanting to parrot-nap this dowdy gray bird!

As Benny watched, Peanut's cashew-shaped beak (gray) opened and a tongue (gray) revealed itself.

"*Brrrrring! Brrrrring!*" said Peanut the Parrot. "*Brrrrring! Brrrrring!*"

Benny lifted his eyebrows in surprise. *Peanut the Parrot is making the sound of a ringing telephone!* Benny pressed his nose between the brass bars of the cage and carefully examined the bird. It had no wind-up key that Benny could see. No door for batteries. No electric cord, either.

"*Ruff?*" Benny said curiously.

The gray bird rang again. "*Brrrrring! Brrrrring!*"

Benny shook his head so vigorously that his tags jingled. *I'll be darned,* he told himself. He stared a little longer, but the gray bird only blinked again.

Okay, sighed Benny. *We've seen the parrot. We've seen his trick. Now it's time to head to the park for another game of Frisbee!* With a spring in his step, Benny led the way out of the sunroom, through the kitchen, and into the hallway, confident that Rosie and Fran, as usual, would follow.

In the hallway, he looked up over his shoulder. *Rosie?* He looked over his other shoulder. *Fran?*

Rosie? Fran? Benny retraced his steps to the sunroom.

Rosie and Fran were still standing in front of the birdcage, their hands clasped under their chins, huge soppy smiles on their faces.

"*Ruff?*" said Benny. *Girls?*

But Rosie and Fran were not looking in Benny's direction. Rosie's and Fran's eyes were fixed on the parrot.

"Peanut?" said Rosie, smiling a shy smile and wiggling her fingers in the direction of the bird.

"*Brrrrring! Brrrrring!*" the bird answered in a

mechanical sort of way. Peanut flapped his dingy gray wings.

The girls threw back their heads and shrieked in delight.

"It's the parrot!" squealed Fran.

"It's Peanut!" added Rosie.

"Peanut the Parrot can sound like a ringing telephone!"

"Not an imitation . . ."

". . . But the *exact* same sound!"

"Peanut's sooo *cute*!"

"You're pretty cute yourself, Shweetie," Peanut answered, kicking his stumpy gray leg to the side.

As Benny watched in disbelief, Rosie and Fran tumbled to the floor in laughter.

"He can talk!" shrieked Fran.

"He kicked his leg to the side like a little tap dancer!" laughed Rosie.

The parrot somersaulted on his rope and squawked. A gray feather detached itself from the bird's tail and, as Benny watched, wafted slowly to the floor.

Benny eyed the bird.

Had he heard correctly? Did he just hear the girls say the bird was cute?

CUTE? Benny shook his head to loosen up his brains. He stepped closer for a second look.

A puppy is cute, Benny told himself at last. *Or a handsome black dog. A baby, plump and laughing in its pram, is cute. The fluffy white lamb I saw at the petting zoo might, in a pinch, be called cute.*

But this moth-eaten gray bird with wrinkled gray feet? This bird that is losing feathers before my eyes?

Benny braced his feet on the floor and squinted his eyes. He tilted his head left, then tilted his head right. He clenched his eyes shut, then opened them for a fresh look.

Benny barked his protest. *Okay! Let's face it! This bird is NOT CUTE! NOTHING about this bird is cute! Not its beady gray eyes! Not its wrinkled gray feet! Not its knobby gray head! Not its drooping gray tail!*

"You're pretty cute yourself, Shweetie," the bird shrieked loudly.

Didn't you say that already? Benny thought indignantly.

Peanut squawked.

Benny felt something begin to ache in the exact center of his chest. For what brave, loyal, good-hearted Benny Bensky saw was this: He saw his dearest Rosie and his darling Fran lying flat on their backs, looking straight at the ugly gray bird, laughing and pedaling their legs joyously into the air.

Another gray feather drifted through the air like a dirty gum wrapper on a cold windy day.

"*Brrrrring! Brrrrring!*" the ugly gray bird shrieked, dancing on his rope. "*Brrrrring! Brrrrring!* You're pretty cute yourself, Shweetie!"

The noise was so loud, the commotion so great, Benny couldn't tell what hurt most. His head? Or his heart?

A Dime a Dozen

"**M**rs. Graham's parrot rings like a telephone!" called Rosie as she, Fran, and Benny banged through the front door of the Perogy Palace and headed toward the kitchen in the back. "Mrs. Graham's parrot sounds exactly like a real ringing telephone!"

But inside the swinging door to the kitchen, Rosie, Fran, and Benny did not see Mr. and Mrs. Bensky. Where could they be? A large vat of hot water steamed on the stove. A bag of onions lay on the cutting board. A bowl of cooked potatoes cooled near the window. Mr. and Mrs. Bensky were nowhere to be seen.

"Mum? Dad?" Rosie called anxiously.

"Over here, kids," called a tired-sounding Mr. Bensky.

The children looked behind them and found Rosie's parents sitting quietly at a table in the very back of the dining area, along with Police Officer Sue and Police Officer Sam.

"You would never believe your ears, Mr. Bensky!" grinned Fran, running over to the table where the grown-ups were seated. "Mrs. Graham's parrot said, 'You're pretty cute yourself, Shweetie!'"

"It's a real live, talking parrot!" added Rosie, hopping up and down with excitement. "You wouldn't believe your ears!"

"Or your eyes!" added Fran.

Mr. Bensky rubbed his bald head with the palms of his hands. He was wearing his white cook's apron. "Nice. That's nice, kids," he said quietly. Then he rubbed his head again and sighed.

"Your father and I *are* interested, girls," Mrs. Bensky explained. "But Daddy is worried just now."

"Worried?" echoed Rosie, suddenly looking worried herself.

"You may have heard," Police Officer Sue explained, leaning toward them and speaking in a low confidential voice, "there have been a number of parrot-nappings around town. I advise you girls to be extremely vigilant of that parrot's well-being." Police Officers Sue and Sam were dressed in their usual blue uniforms, and Police Officer Sue's blue cap rested beside the cup of coffee in front of her.

"The parrot-nappings are a disaster for the Smith Falls Theater Festival," explained Rosie's mother.

"How so?" said Rosie, raising her eyebrows.

"What's the connection?" Fran asked in her frank, logical way.

"People are calling in droves to cancel their reservations for the theater festival," explained Police Officer Sam. "They've heard about the parrot-nappers. I guess you can't blame them. Who wants to vacation in a crime-ridden area?"

"They're scared off by what they read in the papers!" added Mr. Bensky. "And all those people who were coming to the Smith Falls Theater Festival? Why, those exact same people were planning to eat their lunches right here in the Perogy Palace!"

"It's a major loss for us," said Mrs. Bensky. "It puts us out-of-pocket. We've already bought the supplies to feed all those people: flour, cottage cheese, potatoes, butter."

"My sister's bed and breakfast is suffering too," explained Police Officer Sam. "She was booked solid with people all excited about seeing *Hamlet* and all the other plays, but now, cancellations everywhere."

Benny's furry black head turned from right to left, then left to right, as he took in the seriousness of the situation.

"But how are we supposed to get a handle on it?" asked Police Officer Sam. "Parrot-nappings aren't something we learned about in the police academy. We're totally unprepared for something like this! Our handcuffs don't even fit the average parrot!"

"I wouldn't have thought it was the parrot you'd need to handcuff," pointed out Mr. Bensky.

"True," admitted Police Officer Sam, ducking down into his collar, his cheeks pink.

"Be that as it may," said Police Officer Sue. "This is, without a doubt, the strangest case we've ever seen. Parrot-napping? It's unheard of! We don't have a single clue to go on!"

"And even if we manage to recover the parrots, I doubt that they'll be able to tell us anything. . . ."

". . . But parrots *can* talk!" Rosie interrupted. "Mrs. Graham's parrot can talk!"

"Oh, sure," said Police Officer Sam. "You told us. Parrots can often parrot out a few words. A lot of parrots will do that."

"Please let us help you solve the mystery!" said Fran excitedly.

"We want to!" echoed Rosie.

"*RUFF!*" Benny added, bouncing to his feet, the hair on his shoulders almost bristling with excitement. For Benny loved mysteries, even mysteries involving parrots. "*RUFF!*" He looked eagerly from Police Officer Sue's face to Police Officer Sam's face.

"Thanks, guys," said Police Officer Sam. "I accept with thanks. We'll certainly take all the help we can get."

Benny, who loved shaking hands, extended his paw and Police Officer Sam shook it. When Police Officer Sam let go, Benny lifted his paw again and shook the officer's hand a second time. Then Benny held out his paw for a third handshake.

"That's enough, Benny," said Rosie, who had often reminded Benny that you only had to shake hands once.

"First things first," said Fran.

Rosie pulled a small notepad from her pocket and Benny dashed to retrieve a pencil from the pencil jar beside the cash register. He poked his nose up to watch what Rosie wrote.

"Exactly how many parrots have been parrot-napped in Smith Falls?" asked Fran in her crisp businesslike manner.

"Latest count, seven," said Police Officer Sue.

"Seven parrots," Fran said, nodding her head in a professional way as Rosie jotted the information down.

"All were stolen from *Birds-R-Us* down the street," elaborated Police Officer Sam. "Two parrots were parrot-napped Monday morning, another on Tuesday afternoon, then four more Wednesday night."

"Why would anyone steal a parrot?" asked Fran. "I mean, what do you think the *motive* might be for this crime?"

"My best guess is that some person or group has stolen the parrots in order to sell them on the black market," said Police Officer Sue.

Black market? Benny frowned. *Black market?* Benny's doggie mind pictured the local farmers' market with stands and umbrellas and vegetables, all of it, cauliflowers and carrots, spray-painted black.

Police Officer Sue noticed the puzzled look on Benny's face. "By black market, we mean the illegal sale of stolen goods," she explained. "Parrots are worth a lot of money. A single parrot can be sold for a thousand dollars or more."

"A thousand dollars!" yelped Mr. Bensky. "Are you *sure*? Benny here is much bigger, and dogs like Benny are a dime a dozen!"

I am bigger! I'm a lot bigger! Benny thought, standing up and puffing out his chest to show off his size. *How can I be worth less than a single parrot?*

"No, Daddy! That can't be true!" said Rosie, bending down to pull Benny close to her. "Benny can't be worth just . . . well, less than one penny!"

"Benny's worth more than eight-tenths of a cent!" added Fran, who was quick with numbers. She bent down to hug Benny from the other side.

"We think that because Benny's *our* dog," smiled Mrs. Bensky. "To us, Benny is *priceless!* But to someone else it might be different."

". . . To someone else, and on the open market, he's worth nothing, or next to nothing," said Mr. Bensky. He patted Benny's head and grinned sympathetically at him. "Sad but true, my friend."

"The whole thing is that parrots are *exotic pets*," Police Officer Sam explained. "This isn't their natural habitat. They require special care and special handling."

Like me! Benny thought, looking about at the circle of faces. *I need special care too!* Benny couldn't believe, open market or not, he was worth less than one penny!

"It takes a lot of work to raise a good pet parrot," explained Police Officer Sue. "From the time the egg is laid to the time you have a full-grown, healthy, hand-tamed, possibly even *talking* parrot ready for sale."

"Mrs. Graham's parrot *is* a talking parrot!" Rosie eagerly interjected again.

"That makes it all the more valuable," said Police Officer Sam.

"That makes it all the more attractive to people like those coldhearted parrot-nappers," pointed out Police Officer Sue.

"Better take good care of that parrot, girls!" said Rosie's father. "There's no way I want to replace a bird that costs a thousand dollars! Ha, ha, ha!"

"Or more," said Police Officer Sam. "A parrot can cost as much as a diamond ring."

"Or a wide-screen plasma television," said Police Officer Sue.

Benny flopped sadly to the restaurant floor. He rested his chin on his paws.

It had been a day chock-full of surprises.

Number one, Benny Bensky was surprised how ugly a parrot could be. Number two, he was surprised that some people could find an ugly bird "cute." Number three, Benny was completely, totally, and utterly flabbergasted to find out that an ugly, annoying, moulting, gray bird could be worth more (a whole lot more) than a big, smart, handsome, black dog. (A dog with a great nose and superlative detective skills!) *Who would have thought it? Any of it?*

Rosie wrote rapidly on her small notepad, then looked up at everyone. "You'll have to excuse us," she said. "Fran and Benny and I have a few investigations to make."

"Kids!" called out Mr. Bensky. "Have a plate of perogies before you go!"

But Benny, Rosie, and Fran had already left the Perogy Palace, no-nonsense expressions on their faces, and, by unspoken agreement, they were already headed toward the local bird store, *Birds-R-Us*.

Suspect Number one

"It was a terrible shock, going over to say hello to my parrots and finding them missing." Mrs. Russo, owner of *Birds-R-Us*, stood in front of the now empty parrot cages, explaining the situation to Rosie, Fran, and Benny. "I raised those parrots from the time they were hatched. I fed them by hand. I sang to them. I talked to them. They were my babies."

Benny held his nose high, taking in the smells of the store. First, there was the feathery, musty, parrot-y smell of the parrot cages (very much the way Peanut smelled). Next, there was the flowery perfume

Mrs. Russo was wearing (Gardenia? Lime Blossom?). Then, there was something much *much* nicer than either of these smells.

Benny threaded his way toward the scent until he finally arrived at the cash register.

Ah-ha! Just as I thought! There lay a bologna sandwich, already thoughtfully cut into quarters. And before thinking twice (sometimes it was best not to think twice!), Benny opened his mouth, scooped up all four pieces, shut his mouth, and swallowed. *Yum!* Benny carefully licked off the last few crumbs.

Heaps of parrot toys and bags of packing material lay on the floor in the middle of the store, for Rosie and Benny and Fran had arrived just as Mrs. Russo and her assistant were unpacking a shipment of parrot paraphernalia.

"But, how would the parrot-napper know how to take proper care of the parrots?" asked Rosie with a worried frown.

"That's the problem exactly!" Mrs. Russo said, raking her hands through her bright yellow hair. "Parrots are *not* easy to care for! Each one is different. They're like babies – not surprising, when you consider they *are* babies! Baby parrots! Nipper loves grapes if they're cut down the middle, but won't touch a whole grape no matter what! And Napper won't eat grapes, either cut or whole, but gobbles up baby carrots. Noo-Noo is the fussiest. Nothing but the freshest bananas for him! And Noodle, Nelly, Natch, and Norma? Well, they're an entirely different story. Noodle, Nelly, Natch, and Norma love peanuts and melon balls!"

Benny walked over to look at the colored wooden balls and the pretty swings that were still taking up so much space on the floor.

Why do parrots need to have so many toys? Benny asked himself crossly. *Why can't parrots be happy with a tennis ball, a stick, and a plastic hot dog, like me?*

"Were the parrot cages locked at all times, Mrs. Russo?" asked Fran.

"Of course! JP always locks the cages before he leaves for the evening. Don't you, JP?"

"Sure do!" Mrs. Russo's assistant looked up for the first time from the bags of parrot seed he was putting away on the shelves. He was the teenaged boy Benny, Rosie, and Fran had, just this morning, seen at the park; the boy with curly black hair and the T-shirt decorated with a skull and crossbones.

No wonder this boy already knew about the parrot-nappings, Benny thought. *He works in the very store where the parrot-nappings took place!*

"I always lock the cages, but it didn't help us much in this case," explained JP, pointing to ragged holes in the wire cages. "The parrot-napper just cut the wire and took the parrots that way!"

"Do you have any idea – any idea at all – who might have taken the parrots?" asked Fran.

Mrs. Russo pressed a bejeweled finger to her lips while she considered this question. She shook her head. "I worry about it though. What if the parrot-nappers come back? What if they come back for parrot toys and other supplies this time? Parrot-nappers must not be the nicest people. What if they come with a *gun*?"

"A *gun*?" echoed Fran.

"I hope not!" squealed Rosie, jumping back.

BANG! A sound like a shot rang out inside the store.

Benny whirled around, jumping protectively toward Rosie. BAM! BANG! BANG! POW! BANG!

"Yikes! *Help!*" screamed Rosie and Fran. They flung up their arms and leapt about with fright.

BANG! POP! BANG! Again, the sounds of popping and banging filled the store, along with the sound of laughter, "Ha-ha-ha-ha-ha!"

"No! Stop!" begged Mrs. Russo. "Stop! Please stop jumping!"

But Benny leapt about again as more sounds rang in his ears. POP! BANG! POW!

"Stop! Don't you see what you're doing?" said Mrs. Russo. "STOP jumping! You're wrecking my bubble wrap!" Mrs. Russo pointed down at the floor.

Rosie, Fran, and Benny looked down. A large sheet of bubble wrap from the boxes of parrot toys was, indeed, flattened beneath their feet on the floor.

"Oh," said Rosie in a very small voice.

"I was going to use that bubble wrap to send a gift to my sister's pet parrot in Moose Jaw," said Mrs. Russo crossly.

"Ha-ha-ha-ha!" gasped JP, who had collapsed on the floor in laughter. "They jumped around and popped the bubble wrap! They scared themselves! Ha-ha-ha-ha-ha!" Tears of laughter were running down his pale cheeks. "You guys are pretty jumpy for detectives! Maybe you should change your line of work! Maybe you should become librarians! Unless the sound of turning pages is too noisy for you!"

"I'm sorry, Mrs. Russo," said Fran, stepping off the ruined bubble wrap and tiptoeing to the front door of the store.

"We didn't mean to pop your bubble wrap," said Rosie.

Benny scurried toward the door along with Rosie, his shoulders up around his ears, his tail between his legs. *I think we're pretty well finished here!* he told himself.

"Don't forget your detective notepad," called JP with a broad grin.

"No! Don't come for it!" said Mrs. Russo, holding her palm in the air like a traffic policeman. "Stay right where you are! I'll bring it to you. What happened to my bologna sandwich by the way?"

"The dog ate it," grinned JP. "It sort of happened in a flash."

"That was my lunch!" said Mrs. Russo sharply. She retrieved the notepad and pencil, then handed it to Rosie.

When the three detectives stepped out, they heard Mrs. Russo close the door firmly behind them.

"It wasn't very nice for JP to laugh at us," said Rosie, as the three friends walked from *Birds-R-Us* toward Mrs. Graham's house.

Especially when we were trying to concentrate on our detective work, thought Benny crossly.

"It wasn't very funny to make that joke about librarians either," added Fran. "I *like* librarians. Librarians are cool."

"Maybe *he's* the parrot-napper," said Rosie. "He works right in the store. It would be easy for *him*."

"He kind of grins when he talks about the parrot-napper. Did you notice that, Rosie? It's all one big joke to him!"

Benny suddenly sat down on the sidewalk. He

studied a sign on the other side of the road. A two-word sign. Two words he'd seen somewhere before.

"Come on, Benny," said Rosie, tugging gently at his leash.

But Benny refused to budge. He continued to stare at the sign across the street. "*Ruff!*" he said, trying to draw the girls' attention to it.

"Look!" said Rosie, pointing at the shadowy old building across the street. "That's weird. That place that Benny's looking at is called The Liar," said Rosie. "Who would name their building The *Liar*?"

"L-A-I-R," said Fran, spelling the letters of the sign out loud. "That sign doesn't spell *Liar*. It spells *Lair*. You know, like a pirate's lair. A secret hideout."

"Oh," said Rosie.

"That must be the place where JP plays the drums. Remember? He plays drums for that band called The Pirates. Boy, it's pretty amazing that you spotted it, Benny."

"He's a real detective," said Rosie. "Like us. Listen! I've got it! I've got it!" Rosie's eyes shone and her coppery curls danced around her face. She held one finger in the air. "JP's band is called The Pirates, right?"

"Right," said Fran.

"Think about it," said Rosie excitedly. "What do pirates need?"

"Pirate hats?" said Fran.

"What else?"

"Eye patches?"

"*And? And?* Think hard, Fran!"

"Hooks?" said Fran, who was holding one foot up and hopping about on the other. "Wooden legs?"

"What else?"

"Swords? Cutlasses? Oh! Oh! Oh!" Fran clapped her hands together. "I get it, Rosie, I get it! *Pirates need parrots!*"

Rosie, Fran, and Benny danced about, the girls laughing, Benny yelping with excitement.

"Let's look inside!"

The three detectives looked right, then left, then crossed the road to The Lair.

"What kind of place is this?" whispered Fran, as they pressed their noses (two pink and one black) to the window.

"It's a pub. People drink beer and listen to music," said Rosie. "You have to go in with a grown-up."

"They've got chairs and tables," said Fran.

"Look over there," said Rosie. "A stage with a microphone and a set of drums!"

"Hey!" whispered Fran, pointing to a long horizontal rack on stage. "Look, Rosie!"

"A parrot's perch!" Rosie whispered back.

"It's long enough for a dozen parrots!" The three friends looked at each other.

Rosie pulled out her notepad and Benny and Fran huddled around it. Benny's tail thumped against the chipped black window frame. He knew what Rosie was going to write, but he wanted to watch her write it anyway.

Rosie turned to a brand-new page, clutched the stubby pencil firmly between her fingers, then, in very neat handwriting, wrote the following words: *Suspect Number One: JP (Birds-R-Us).*

So Long, Peanut

Cushions from the pale-green couch in Mrs. Graham's sunroom lay scattered everywhere. An African violet that had been blooming by the window was strewn across the floor. Shreds of newsprint were scattered across the cushions, the floor, and the coffee table.

"Hello, Shmartie pants!" screeched Peanut from the top of the doorframe in the sunroom. "Come on in!"

Benny stared at the mess Peanut had made, his mouth open with shock.

"Uh-oh," said Fran. "Peanut opened the latch on his cage."

"Oh, dear," said Rosie. "He tore up the phone book."

"This poor plant!" said Fran shaking her head. "What a mess."

Benny looked up at Rosie and Fran, then back at Peanut.

At last! thought Benny. *This will show them! At last Rosie and Fran will see what a nuisance Peanut really is!*

Benny raised one brown eyebrow as he watched Rosie and Fran pick up the velvet cushions, fluff them up, and replace them on the couch. He continued to watch while Rosie dropped to her knees to pick up the shreds of paper, and Fran went to get a broom and dustpan to sweep up the African violet.

Aren't they going to say anything? Anything at all? Benny asked himself. *Isn't that dumb bird going to get into any kind of trouble?*

"Hey, Rosie!" said Fran.

Benny looked Fran's way expectantly.

"Why don't we let Peanut the Parrot join our detective team?"

"Good idea, Fran," said Rosie. "We could teach him to say, 'Hands up, you parrot-napping varmint! Yes! I mean you!' Wouldn't that be great?"

Rosie and Fran threw back their heads and laughed aloud.

Benny stared.

"We could make him a little detective cap, with a little visor and a little star on it!" said Fran.

"He would look *so* cute!"

"Say it, Peanut," said Fran. "Say, 'Hands up, you parrot-napping varmint! Yes! I mean you!'"

"You're pretty cute yourself, Shweetie!" shrieked Peanut from the coffee table.

Benny watched, his jaw hanging open in surprise. He felt as stunned as if someone had whacked him with a rolled-up newspaper. He looked left and right, then climbed quietly onto the pale-green couch to think.

When I was a puppy (A tiny puppy! A smart puppy! An adorable puppy!), I also tipped a plant out of a pot. What happened? Why, everyone yelled at me and sent me to obedience school!

BUT! When Peanut tips a plant out of a pot (PLUS tears up the phone book, PLUS scatters the cushions), what happens to Peanut? Why, Rosie and Fran want to promote him to the detective squad!

TO THE DETECTIVE SQUAD?

Benny scowled while Rosie pulled paper and tape from her backpack and Fran went off in search of scissors.

It's NOT fair! Benny told himself. *It's not right! The detective squad? What has Peanut done to earn a place on the detective squad? Peanut is a pest! Peanut will ruin everything!*

"These are kitchen scissors," said Fran, coming back in, "but they should work. What are you doing on the couch, Benny?"

"Off the couch, Benny," said Rosie, turning around and sternly pointing to the floor.

. "Bad dog, Benny! Off the couch," said Fran, also pointing to the floor.

. Reluctantly, Benny slipped his front legs off the couch.

Okay, look at me, Benny's face innocently read. *I'm off.* He looked directly into Rosie's face, his belly and back legs still resting on the comfy velvet couch.

Rosie craned her neck up to get a good look at Benny's back legs. "All the way! I mean it, Benny!" she commanded (for Benny had tried this trick once or twice before).

Darn! With a reluctant groan, Benny slipped his back legs off the couch as well.

"Peanut will be *so* cute!" laughed Rosie, turning her attention back to the paper detective cap they were making for Peanut.

Benny strolled into the kitchen where Peanut was now pecking at his dowdy gray reflection in the door of the stainless-steel refrigerator.

"Yoo-hoo! Come on in!" squawked Peanut, walking along the edge of the kitchen counter. "That's right, Shmartie pants!" he yelled, hopping down to sit on the upright lid of the open garbage can.

"Peanut will look so important!" Benny could hear Fran saying. "Let's put the little star right here."

"It will bring out the blue of his eyes," agreed Rosie happily.

The blue of his eyes! thought Benny. He felt a rumble come to his throat. *Peanut does NOT have blue eyes! Peanut has GRAY eyes! Everything about Peanut – top to bottom – is dull, murky, and gray!*

Benny looked at Peanut, looked at the open lid of the garbage can, then looked over his shoulder toward the sunroom where the girls were happily talking and laughing, cutting and pasting.

Benny walked very quietly up behind Peanut. He moved up so close, Benny could smell the feathery parrot smell of Peanut. He could smell the sunflower seeds and the banana the girls had given the parrot earlier.

With the gentlest bunt of his nose – *BOOP!* – as casually as if he'd done it accidentally, Benny tipped the parrot into the garbage can. Then, with a quick scoop of his large black paw – *WHOMP!* – Benny slammed down the lid.

Benny lowered his head and butted the closed garbage can into the broom closet. Then, hastily, Benny pushed the door of the broom closet shut with his large black nose.

CLICK.

Benny looked about. *That's better,* he told himself.

In the sunroom, Rosie and Fran were still cutting and pasting.

Benny hummed a tune to himself, then did a little dance step right there on the shiny kitchen floor.

So long, Peanut, so long!
So long, Peanut, all gone!

Now we can proceed with some serious detective work, thought Benny. *But first, a brief nap!*

He sauntered back to the sunroom, stretched in a lazy way, then spread himself out on the floor; his head against Rosie's thigh, his toes pressing down on Fran's leg. Rosie stopped pasting for a moment to scratch Benny behind his ears and into the thick ruff around his neck. Benny groaned with pleasure, then rolled over onto his back, his four black legs flopping lazily in the air.

Summer! thought Benny, as he drifted off. *Hanging out with my best friends. What could be more agreeable?*

The same little tune ran dreamily through Benny's head,

So long, Peanut, so long!
So long, Peanut, all gone!

The phone rang – the real phone – and Rosie answered it.

"Alright, Mummy," Benny heard Rosie say. "Can Fran eat over? Oh, goody!" She clattered the receiver down. "Fran! We're eating early because Mummy and Daddy are going to a rehearsal. If your mum says yes, you can eat supper with us!"

"My basket is full," said Fran. "Do you want me to help you with yours, Rosie?"

From where Benny lay digesting the tasty hamburger (which he'd eaten with a dab of ketchup), he could see Fran's wicker basket overflowing with puffy white Kleenex flowers, while Rosie's basket was still almost empty.

"How do you do them so fast?" Rosie asked, pushing up her glasses and looking at the small, lop-sided, lumpy Kleenex flower in the palm of her hand.

"Remember what your mum said? If we cut the Kleenexes ahead of time, it will go faster."

As Benny and Rosie watched, Fran deftly cut two Kleenexes down the middle. Then she laid them in a pile, four Kleenexes thick. She pleated across the length of the Kleenexes, fastened an elastic band several times around the middle, then fluffed out the Kleenex petals, eight layers on each side.

"*Voila!*" said Fran, holding her perfect flower up for Rosie and Benny to admire.

"Yours are nice," said Rosie.

"Maybe yours just needs a bit more fluffing," said Fran. "Here, I'll help you. It's going to be fun, isn't it, Rosie? Wearing our white dresses and throwing our white flowers each time someone gets murdered."

"How come so many people have to get murdered anyway?" complained Rosie.

"It's the way the play goes. Hamlet – I mean, your dad – kills quite a few of them, I think."

"With that old egg flipper?" asked Rosie irritably.

"Of course not! He's just practicing with an egg flipper. In the play, he will be using a real sword. Look! We've finished! Now your basket is full of white Kleenex flowers too."

It was true. Both baskets were overflowing with fluffy white Kleenex flowers. They looked real. If it didn't involve standing up, Benny would have been tempted to go over and smell one.

"Well, thank goodness," said Rosie, standing up

and adjusting her glasses again. "Because we have to go check Peanut's food and water. Come on, guys."

Again? thought Benny. He burped up the homey scent of hamburger and onions. *Didn't we already check on that dumb bird twice today?*

Benny staggered to his feet and followed Rosie and Fran back to Mrs. Graham's house. Rosie and Fran went directly to Peanut's cage and looked inside, expectant smiles on their faces.

"Peanut?" they said together, then looked at each other questioningly.

"Oh no! Peanut's gone!" said Rosie.

"Peanut's been parrot-napped!" shrieked Fran.

"Peanut?" said Rosie, still staring at the empty cage.

"What are we going to do, Rosie? What will Mrs. Graham say?"

"Wait! Did we put him back before we went to supper, Fran? I don't remember putting him back in his cage."

"Then maybe he's still here! Peanut? *Pea*-nut?"

"The doors and windows are closed. I don't see any signs of a parrot-napper breaking in."

Rosie and Fran checked the top of the doorframe where Peanut liked to perch. They checked the stainless-steel refrigerator in the kitchen where Peanut liked to admire himself. They checked under the couch and along the curtain rods. They checked everywhere they could think of.

"Peanut?" Rosie called. "Peanut!"

"Say something, Peanut," begged Fran.

Benny sipped a cooling drink of water from his dish in the kitchen, then strolled into the sunroom. The pale-green couch stretched like a soft spring lawn before him. Quietly, he placed his front legs up on the soft velvet cushions, then pulled up his back legs too. He felt his large furry body slip deep into the soft velvet cushions.

Comfty!

"Say something, Peanut!" he heard the girls call.

Benny, drifting off to sleep, dreamt he told Rosie and Fran that Peanut was just fine.

"Where is he, Benny?" Rosie asked in his dream. "Where?"

In his dream, Benny was far away, floating on a soft green cloud. He relaxed his shoulders. He jiggled his hindquarters. He wiggled his toes into the soft green pile of cloud. *Comfty!*

Plastic Hot Dog

"Oh, criminy!" said Mr. Bensky, who'd been called in after rehearsal to look for Peanut. He held his head in his hands and groaned. "How much did Police Officer Sam say a parrot costs? One thousand dollars? I wonder if I could find a cheaper one on eBay?"

"We looked everywhere, Daddy," said Rosie, who was close to tears. "Do you think he's been parrot-napped, Daddy, along with the other parrots?"

"Wait," said Mr. Bensky, holding up his hand. "Listen! Do you hear something?"

From where he dozed on the couch in the sun-room, Benny heard the faintest scratchy, scrambling sound. He sleepily opened his eyes, then shut them again. The scratchy sound came from far away, far away from his green cloud that was so soft and so comfortable.

"That must be Peanut!" he heard Fran say. "I think the sound's coming from the wall!"

"It's muffled," said Mr. Bensky. "I hope that bird didn't get caught inside the furnace pipes."

"The furnace pipes! Oh, Daddy!" said Rosie, biting her bottom lip. "What will happen to Peanut in the furnace pipes?"

"He won't get burnt up, will he Mr. Bensky?" asked Fran.

"I'll tell you what," replied Mr. Bensky. "Let's not panic just yet. Let's find Peanut first. And then, if need be, we'll panic."

From where Benny lay on the couch, he could see Mr. Bensky tapping the kitchen walls and listening for any answering sound with the wineglass he held to his ear. "One thousand dollars," Mr. Bensky muttered.

Then, from somewhere far away, there was a scratching of claws and an outraged squawk.

"Peanut!" called Rosie. "Don't be worried, Peanut! We're coming!"

"We're going through this room inch by inch!" declared Mr. Bensky. "You girls go through every nook and cranny on this side, and I'll go through everything on that side."

Click. Benny heard someone open the broom closet door.

"SQUAAAWK! SQUAAAWK!" came an angry sound.

"We're getting warmer!" called Fran, rummaging through various cleaning supplies. "Peanut's somewhere in the broom closet!"

Benny opened one eye. He looked into the kitchen to see Rosie pressing her toe onto the pedal of the garbage can. A rumpled gray parrot crawled out and perched on the edge of the can.

"Oh, Peanut! Oh, baby!" said Rosie, putting her hand out so Peanut could step onto it. "Sweetheart! We were so worried!"

What's with this "baby," "sweetheart" business? thought Benny, listening from the couch.

"How did you get in there, you little monkey?" laughed Fran, running her hands over Peanut's feathers.

Peanut hopped from Rosie's wrist to Fran's shoulder. "Bad dog, Benny!" Peanut shouted. "Off the couch, Benny! Off the couch! Bad dog!"

Suddenly, everyone – Rosie, Fran, Mr. Bensky, and Peanut – were in the sunroom and glaring down at Benny.

"Isn't that something!" Mr. Bensky chuckled. "Did you hear that bird order Benny off the couch? That bird is smart!"

If that bird is so smart, how come he couldn't get out of the garbage can? Benny thought crossly, slumping to the hard floor in front of the soft couch.

"You can't let that dog on Mrs. Graham's couch, girls," said Mr. Bensky.

"We don't, Mr. Bensky," said Fran.

"We tell him, Daddy."

"Off the couch, Benny!" shrieked Peanut. "Bad dog! Off the couch!"

Again, Mr. Bensky chuckled.

Suddenly, Benny found himself on his feet, barking back at the bird who was clearly too dumb to know he was already off the couch. "WOOF! WOOF! WOOF! WOOF! WOOF!" Benny barked hoarsely. *Don't tell ME what to do, birdbrain!*

"What's going on with you, Benny?" asked Rosie, covering her ears. "Stop that barking!"

But Benny braced his feet on the floor and kept right on barking. He barked so loud, the air trembled. He barked so loud, the copper pots in the kitchen hummed.

"WOOF! WOOF! WOOF!"

"Hey! Cool it!" shouted Mr. Bensky. "I mean it, Benny Bensky!" He grabbed Benny's collar and stared directly into Benny's eyes. Benny blinked, swallowed, then looked at the floor. But the moment Mr. Bensky turned his head, Benny glared darkly up at Peanut. "WOOF! WOOF! WOOF!"

"That's it. You're coming home with me," said Mr. Bensky, grabbing Benny's collar again. "You can cool your heels in the backyard, Mister."

Mr. Bensky flung open the back door of the Bensky house and dragged a reluctant Benny to it. He placed the sole of his shoe on Benny's backside and shoved Benny firmly outside.

"You learn to listen!" thundered Mr. Bensky. He slammed the door with a bang.

Benny hung his head and sighed. He lay down on the back steps beside his plastic hot dog. He thought of Rosie and Fran over at Mrs. Graham's house having fun without him. He thought of the little detective cap they made for that dumb parrot. He thought of how well he and Rosie and Fran worked as a team, how much fun they had, and how the team would be ruined with that birdbrain, Peanut, in it.

Life can be strange, Benny thought to himself. *Things happen that are the opposite of what you expect. Like my plastic hot dog.* The size and shape of the hot dog made it look absolutely like a real hot dog. The reddish-brown color, the sheen on the edges where the light reflected, the way the weiner sat plumply on the bun. Everything about it made his mouth water. Everything about it made him want to grab it between his teeth. But Benny knew what would happen if he tried to eat it.

Benny reached over and sadly poked the hot dog with his nose.

Squeak, went the plastic hot dog.

See? he told himself. Slowly, a country song began to form itself in his head. Benny drew himself back on his haunches and began to sing:

Plastic hot dog, plastic hot dog,
You remind me – of friends of mine!

Who are smart, and who are funny,
But to-day! Like tur-pen-tine!

What's so terrific about having an ugly gray parrot
for a friend? Benny asked himself. *Parrots are no fun!*
The words of the song made Benny feel sadder, but,
strangely, also a bit better.

He looked at the moon that was starting to show
its wan face in the sky. Benny threw back his head and
sang the song a few more times.

7

Dog-Gone!

Not a drop of milk nor a single egg was to be found in the Bensky refrigerator the next morning, so everyone (including Fran) trooped down to the Perogy Palace to have breakfast before the restaurant officially opened.

This was Benny's favorite way to eat at the Perogy Palace, with the *SORRY, WE'RE CLOSED* sign on the door, their own happy group eating delicious perogies at the large round table in the back, nearest the kitchen. Benny finished the meat-filled perogies from his personal bowl on the floor, looked up, and wagged his tail.

"Don't look at me, Benny," said Mrs. Bensky, "I'm eating my own breakfast now."

Police Officer Sue and Police Officer Sam tapped at the window with hopeful grins on their faces.

"What say we let these poor fellas in for a cup of coffee?" grinned Mr. Bensky, opening the door for them.

Fran and Rosie waited while Mr. Bensky settled Police Officers Sue and Sam at the round family table. Then Fran cleared her throat and asked politely, "Any progress on the parrot-napping case, Police Officer Sue and Police Officer Sam?"

"Not too much from our end," said Police Officer Sue, biting into her cheese and potato-filled perogies. "Gosh these make a perfect breakfast! How about you?"

"We investigated over at *Birds-R-Us,*" explained Rosie, bringing out the detective notepad that she carried everywhere. "We have the name of one suspect." She opened her book to the Suspect Page, and showed everyone what she had written. *Suspect Number One: JP (Birds-R-Us).*

"JP? That boy who works at the pet store?" said Police Officer Sue, pushing her breakfast away and listening carefully. "What makes him a suspect in the parrot-napping case?"

Rosie, Benny, and Fran looked at each other.

"He sort of . . ." said Fran.

". . . He *laughed* at us when we were investigating," said Rosie, with a sudden stubborn tilt of her chin. "Plus, we saw a parrot perch in the place where he plays drums in his band."

"You did?" said Police Officers Sue and Sam, leaning forward and speaking in unison.

"Yes. And we're pretty sure it means he also has the parrots!"

"Mind you," said Police Officer Sue, "parrots can perch on almost anything. It's the parrots we're interested in, not the actual parrot perch."

"But!" said Fran. She held her forefinger importantly in the air. "What I mean to say is . . ." Everyone turned to her, waiting for more, but after a moment, Fran only put her finger down again.

"Fran's right!" said Rosie. "I mean, she's probably right. We don't have proof yet, but JP is definitely a suspect."

Benny listened carefully to each of the speakers. He looked again at what Rosie had written on the Suspect Page. *If only,* thought Benny, *we had a few more names on that list!*

"Do you think a parrot could help track down the parrot-napper?" asked Fran, swallowing the last piece of her strawberry perogy (which she'd eaten with a generous amount of melted butter and sour cream). She wiped her lips on the edge of her T-shirt. "I mean, we were thinking the parrot we are parrot-sitting would make a good addition to our detective team."

Benny sat up straight, his eyes blinking rapidly, and waited for Police Officers Sue and Sam to reply.

"A parrot?" said Police Officer Sam, pouring himself another cup of coffee from the pot on the table. "Gosh. I don't know." He added two teaspoons of sugar, then thoughtfully clinked his spoon in the cup. "Never heard of anyone using a parrot to solve a crime."

"What special talents does this parrot have?" asked Police Officer Sue.

"Peanut can talk!" Rosie answered eagerly. "Peanut can say all kinds of things!"

"Right now," explained Fran excitedly, "we're teaching him to say, 'Hands up, you parrot-napping varmint! Yes, I mean you!'"

"Wouldn't that be great to help solve the parrot-napping mystery?" asked Rosie. "When we catch the parrot-napper, Peanut can say, 'Hands up, you parrot-napping varmint! Yes, I mean you!'"

"Could be," Police Officer Sue said, looking doubtful. She poured herself another cup of coffee. "Hard to say. But why would I need a parrot to say that for me? I could say that myself. If I knew who to say it *to*, that is."

"Now! A *dog* is a different story!" said Police Officer Sam. "With a dog like Benny Bensky, you've got yourself a real detective. He's smart. He's loyal. He's got superlative hearing. He can read body language better than most humans."

Benny leapt up, placing his front paws on the edge of the table, his eyes fastened on Police Officer Sam's.

"And sense of smell! Don't forget sense of smell!" said Police Officer Sue. "A dog's sense of smell is fifty times as good as yours or mine."

Yes-Siree! thought Benny, his paws still on the edge of the table. *Now you're talking! YUP! YUP! YUP! Go on!*

"Hey! Stop that barking, Benny," rumbled Mr. Bensky. "This is a restaurant, not a back alley. And get your paws off the table, Mister!" He took Benny's collar and pulled him back so that Benny stood on all fours again.

"We don't know what gets into him sometimes," apologized Mrs. Bensky. "He just starts barking out of the blue lately."

"Did you say a dog smells *fifty times* as good as us?" said Rosie. "I knew Benny could smell really well, but that's, like, *incredibly, amazingly, unbelievably* well!"

"Exactly!" said Police Officer Sue. "You know the way you or I can smell these wonderful perogies or this coffee? Especially when we walk into a place? A dog's whole life is like that. He lives in a sea of smells! He smells you, he smells me, he smells the person who was sitting here last night."

"Plus whatever is in their pockets!" added Police Officer Sam with a grin. "That's why dogs are used worldwide to battle crime, find lost people, detect drugs, locate explosives and all other types of contraband."

Police Officer Sue took the salt shaker and sprinkled a bit of salt on the table. "Look at that," she said.

"See all those grains of salt? Quite a few, aren't there? That's how many sensors we have in our noses to pick up smells." Everyone stared at the tiny pile of salt on the table. "Now," said Police Officer Sue, "look at the rest of the salt in the shaker." Everyone's eyes, including Benny's, turned to the column of white salt crystals in the nearly full salt shaker. "That's how many sensors our friend Benny has got to smell with."

"*Wow!*" said Rosie, staring down at the tiny bit of salt on the table, then at the large amount of salt in the salt shaker. She looked at Benny with huge admiring eyes. "*Ben-ny Ben-sky!* You're really something! You're terrific!"

Fran reached down and stroked him all the way from his nose to his tail. "You're amazing, Benny," she said.

Benny stood tall, his tail curled up above his back, and allowed himself to be admired. *It's true,* he thought. *Everything Police Officers Sue and Sam said is true. I love to smell! Smelling is fun! Take now for example.* He lifted his large black nose in the air. First, there was that maddeningly wonderful smell he could not get enough of – *butter! butter! buttery butter!* – and he glanced longingly at the table. *Meat! Cheese! Sour cream! There is no end of smells!*

And how interesting all the humans smell as well! How endlessly intriguing each one is! Rosie, for example, smells slightly of sweet peas and chocolate and what else? Why, she also smells of cotton pajamas. While Fran, on the other hand, smells of gingersnaps and jelly beans. Mr. Bensky is sweaty and salty – sometimes a bit like an old fish! – while Mrs. Bensky smells a bit more of oranges and wood. Police Officer Sam has a leathery, manly smell. Police Officer Sue? Why, she smells of soap and wool!

Police Officer Sue's cell phone rang, and Benny heard her end of the conversation.

"Billy Bittle the Barber's parrots have been stolen? I see. Both of them?"

"Oh, no!" said Mr. Bensky, the grin dropping from his face. "Not Billy Bittle's parrots too! Not Elmer and Mavis! I adore those birds! That's why I always get my hair cut at Billy Bittle's! Elmer and Mavis are so darned entertaining!"

"Elmer would sing Blue Moon," Billy Bittle explained in his squeaky little voice, "and, Mavis, she would bring up the end by saying, 'Shave and a haircut, six bits!' Those birds were something special! They brought all kinds of customers into the store."

Benny's head rocked back and forth. He felt a little seasick. He had come over with Rosie and Fran to Billy Bittle's barbershop to find out what he could about who had taken the parrots and why. But Benny found he was unable to pull his eyes away from the red, white, and blue stripes on the revolving barber pole. The stripes that went around.

And around.

And around.

Benny couldn't pull his eyes away. He felt like a fly stuck to a piece of flypaper!

"Benny? Are you paying attention?" said Rosie, placing a hand on top of Benny's head and turning it around to face her open detective notepad.

Whew! Benny's eyes snapped away from the barber pole. *At last!*

"Did you find the door forced or the window broken when you came in, Mr. Bittle?" asked Fran, looking around the small barbershop.

"Door wasn't forced, windows weren't broken. Windows don't lock, mind you," Billy Bittle answered in his high-pitched voice. "No reason to lock the window. 'Specially now," Billy Bittle's voice trembled, "with Elmer and Mavis gone."

"My dad really liked Elmer and Mavis, Mr. Bittle," said Rosie kindly. "I hope we can get them back for you."

"I hope so, that's for sure. Guess I never locked the cage either," admitted Billy. "Elmer and Mavis were free to come in and out of their cage as they liked. Liked to sit on my shoulder, sometimes on top of the mirrors or on top of the Lego castle I made for them."

Benny looked admiringly at the large Lego castle Mr. Bittle had built for his birds.

"Who else has a key to your barbershop, Mr. Bittle?" asked Fran crisply, looking over to Rosie who had her pencil poised over her notepad.

"No one," said Billy Bittle, scratching his head. "It's a small operation. I do everything myself. Except the entertainment, that is. Elmer and Mavis took care of that end."

"Did you have many customers yesterday?" asked Rosie.

"Well, pret' near everyone was in yesterday," yelled Billy Bittle. "Lots of excitement about the play, you know. Your dad was in, Rosie, and a whole bunch of the other actors, sword-fighters and all. Bet it's gonna be good. Me and the Missus are going, that's for sure.

Even if out-of-towners are canceling. Director was in, too. He was the last customer. Very refined gentleman. Just squeezed him in before I locked up for the night."

"Mr. Bellefleur," said Rosie, jotting down this information.

"That's right. Mr. Bellefleur. Cuts a fine figure with his red cape."

"Did anyone take any special interest in Elmer and Mavis?" asked Fran.

"Everyone takes an interest. That's the whole charm of Elmer and Mavis. Everyone loves those birds." Billy Bittle stopped to blow his nose.

Benny paced the floor checking for clues, for smells. *Hair lotion. Peppermints. Leather.*

Benny lifted his paws to the windowsill on the back wall and looked out. *Well, well,* thought Benny. He turned to Rosie.

"What do you see out there, Benny?" asked Rosie, coming over.

"Look! It's JP!" said Fran. "He's reading a comic book in the hammock. I didn't know JP was your neighbor, Mr. Bittle."

"Oh, yes. Nice boy, even though he could use a haircut," giggled Mr. Bittle.

"*Hmmmm,*" said Fran, carefully noncommittal. "Was JP ever interested in Elmer and Mavis, Mr. Bittle?"

"Real interested. Loves those birds. Comes over all the time. Not for a haircut o'course, though I always offer him a haircut, half-price."

"Do you see what I see, Rosie?" asked Fran.

"I do," said Rosie, jotting down the information in her notepad.

What Rosie wrote was this: *Ladder. In JP's backyard. Tall enough to reach Mr. Bittle's back window.*

"Let's make a list of all the facts we have about the parrot-napping case," said Rosie as she unlocked Mrs. Graham's door.

"Good idea," said Fran, taking the notepad and pencil. "Let's write down everything we know for absolute sure."

The girls sat down with Benny on the sunroom floor.

"Fact number one," said Fran. "Nine parrots have been parrot-napped in Smith Falls."

"Fact number two," said Rosie, "seven parrots were from *Birds-R-Us,* and two were from Billy Bittle's barbershop."

"Fact number three," continued Fran. "By the way, why's it so quiet in here?" She stood up and looked into Peanut's brass cage. "Peanut?"

"What's wrong with Peanut?" asked Rosie.

Both girls were on their feet now, checking the top of the doorframe, the curtain rods, the top of the bookshelf, and behind the couch.

"Oh! I know!" said Rosie happily. She led the way to the kitchen, where she opened the broom closet and stepped on the pedal of the garbage can.

The garbage can flipped open and the three friends stared inside. Except for the banana peel Rosie had left there earlier, the garbage can was empty. There was a long silence.

"That's impossible," said Fran at last.

The three detectives clustered close together and walked from room to room, checking everywhere.

When they reached the small powder room off the front hall, no one spoke. They stared at the broken glass on the floor, at the small gray feather that remained caught on the edge of the torn screen.

Benny stared out the window, his thoughts in a swirl. *Dog-gone,* he thought to himself. *Though, maybe it's more accurate to say bird-gone!*

Benny had thought he would be happy if Peanut

disappeared, but he wasn't. In fact, while he surveyed the crime scene, Benny felt a growl rise in his throat. "*RRRRRRRRRR!*" *This is wrong,* he told himself. *Very wrong.*

Like crime fighters everywhere, Benny longed to put wrongs to right!

Rosie's father, Mr. Bensky, rushed over after work to repair the broken window in Mrs. Graham's powder room.

"What about Peanut, Daddy?" asked Rosie, plaintively. "What do you think the parrot-napper will do with him?"

"Let's just hope the parrot-napper will be caught and the parrots restored to their rightful owners before Mrs. Graham gets back," said Mr. Bensky in a deep rumbly voice. But as he put his tools back in his toolbox, Benny heard him talking quietly to himself. "One thousand dollars? Two thousand dollars? Criminy! If I get a chicken and dye it gray, I wonder whether Mrs. Graham would notice the difference?"

"What if the parrot-napper doesn't know what to feed a parrot?" worried Rosie. "What if he or she doesn't know Peanut needs water? What if they put him in a draft?"

"Parrots get sick if you put them in a draft!" said Fran.

"At this point, all we can do is hope for the best," said Mr. Bensky, sounding far from confident.

"Mrs. Graham is coming back the day after tomorrow, Mr. Bensky," said Fran. "There's only this evening," she said, counting on her fingers, "tomorrow's the play and, then, the next day Mrs. Graham will be back."

"That's only three days," said Rosie with a worried frown. They were locking Mrs. Graham's front door, preparing to go home. "And look, Daddy! It's *already* getting dark!"

"Your old dad can do a lot of things," said Mr. Bensky, "but he can't stop the sun from setting. But, here, sweetheart, I'll try." He reached with both hands toward the sun, which was nestled on the horizon. Mr. Bensky grunted with the effort of trying to budge it upward.

"Joke," he explained.

But no one laughed.

Parrots and Pirates

Benny took his time leaving Mrs. Graham's yard.
He checked around the grass and the flowers.
Was there some clue they had overlooked? When he
smelled the window ledge or the window to the
powder room, he smelled a parrot-y kind of smell –
the way Peanut smelled, for sure – but he couldn't
catch even the smallest whiff of anything else. This
was like trying to put together a jigsaw puzzle without all the pieces!

"Look! What's that?" said Fran, pointing to Mr.
Bellefleur's window.

"What's what?" said Rosie, sadly.

"I saw a wing in Mr. Bellefleur's window!"

"A wing?" said Rosie, brightening. "Are you sure?"

They stopped walking and stared at Mr. Bellefleur's house. There was a light shining in the front window, but the yellow curtains were drawn.

"His curtains are shut," said Rosie. "How could you see a wing?"

"I saw the *shadow* of a wing across the window. You know, like in a spooky movie. It was just this huge wing."

"A parrot's wing?" asked Rosie. "But a parrot's wing is not that huge, Fran."

"The shadow could be huge, though," pointed out Mr. Bensky. "If the parrot's wing was between a source of light and the curtain, well, you see, that could make the shadow huge. Just like if we turn around right here, see?" All four of them turned around to look down the sidewalk. "We're just normal-sized," said Mr. Bensky. "But because of the angle of the sun, our shadows are huge."

Cool! thought Benny, watching his shadow stretching down until it almost reached the community center on the other side of Mrs. Graham's house. He looked at his gigantic shadow, bunched up his shoulders, and growled.

"We look like giants!" said Rosie, doing a little jig. "Look! I'm a dancing giant!"

But Benny had no more time for games. He turned and dashed up Mr. Bellefleur's walk, up his porch steps, and to his front window.

"Wait, Benny!" called Rosie, as she and Fran followed close behind.

The three friends pressed their hands and noses to the glass and peeked in through the crack between the curtains.

"Now, kids," Mr. Bensky cautioned from where he stood on the sidewalk, "we can't just go around peeking in people's windows." He looked both ways, then added to himself, "On the other hand, replacing a parrot is a pretty darn big deal." He ducked down behind the hedge. "See anything interesting?" he asked in a hushed voice.

The three detectives watched through the crack between the curtains a moment longer, then turned back to join Mr. Bensky.

"Nothing," said Rosie with a sigh, "just Mr. Bellefleur, walking back and forth in his living room, talking to himself and swinging his cape around in the air."

"Oh, yeah," said Mr. Bensky. "His cape. Mr. Bellefleur does that quite a lot."

"Do you think it was the corner of Mr. Bellefleur's cape you saw?" said Rosie.

"Maybe," agreed Fran. But she looked over her shoulder at Mr. Bellefleur's backlit curtains again.

Suddenly Rosie stopped walking, bringing Benny to a standstill as well.

Mr. Bensky turned around. "Getting sleepy, sweetheart?" he said to Rosie.

"Daddy," said Rosie. "Daddy, would you please take us to The Lair?"

"You want to go to The Lair?" said Mr. Bensky. "That broken-down, ramshackle pub at the far end of Main Street? But I can't take you sweet innocent kids to a no-good place like that!"

"But, Mr. Bensky!" Fran explained. "Rosie is right! We've got to check it out and we've got to check it out tonight!"

"You've *got* to take us, Daddy!" Rosie begged, tugging on her father's hand. "Peanut is missing, Mrs. Graham comes home the day after tomorrow, and our number one suspect plays drums at The Lair tonight!"

"JP?" said Mr. Bensky. "That kid who works at *Birds-R-Us?* You still think he did it?"

"We saw a parrot perch right on stage, Daddy!" explained Rosie, excitedly. "A really long parrot perch big enough to hold all the missing parrots!"

"You see," Fran added, "JP's band is called The Pirates. . . ."

". . . And Pirates need parrots! Get it, Daddy? We think they put the parrots on the perch when they play their music!"

Mr. Bensky let out a low thoughtful whistle. "A pretty good way of drawing a crowd!" he agreed.

Benny whapped his tail against everyone's legs.

"The whole band wears skull-and-crossbones T-shirts," added Fran.

"We have JP's name written down as suspect number one and everything!" said Rosie.

"*Hmmmm.* I see what you mean," said Mr. Bensky, nodding thoughtfully. "Parrots and pirates." He looked up and grinned. "You know, it all makes sense in a *detective-y* kind of way."

Parrots and pirates, thought Benny, who was leashed

but eagerly leading the way to The Lair. *Parrots and pirates. Yes! Those two go together like peanut butter and jam, like perogies and sour cream!*

Without breaking his stride – for Benny was in the lead and he liked being in the lead – he lunged to the side and scooped up half an ice-cream sandwich that had been dropped on the sidewalk. *Ice-cream sandwich! Yumm! Why, parrots and pirates went together like an ice-cream sandwich,* Benny reflected, still briskly leading the way. *Soft crumbly cookie on the outside, cool creamy ice cream on the inside!*

Benny grinned. *I'm a poet, don't cha know it.*

"It'll be about five minutes, sir," a waiter in a white apron told Mr. Bensky. Benny, Rosie, Fran, and Mr. Bensky were in the lineup waiting for a table at The Lair.

Benny looked around him. He'd never been to such a grown-up place before, but he was pretty sure he was going to like it. There was the promising smell of pizzas and sausages and meat pies. There was laughter and conversation. There were flickering candles on each of the tables, creating a cosy ambiance and also hiding the dust and grime they'd seen earlier.

The candles provided the only lighting, except for the colored spotlights that were already trained on the stage at the front.

The Pirates had not yet begun to play, but everything was ready for them. On the stage were several stools, a stand-up microphone, and a set of drums with a skull and crossbones painted on the side.

"Daddy! See?" whispered Rosie. She pointed to the far side of the stage. "There's the parrot perch we were telling you about!"

Mr. Bensky craned his neck forward to see better. "You're sure that's not just a coat rack? It looks like an ordinary coat rack to me."

"But there are no coats on it, are there, Mr. Bensky?" whispered Fran.

"Mind you, it *is* summer," pointed out Mr. Bensky. His eyes had already located the chalkboard menu on the wall. "The Walk-the-Plank Pizza here looks pretty darn tantalizing, doesn't it?"

"Are you the young ladies who are the flower girls in *Hamlet?*" It was a pleasant male voice. Rosie, Fran, and Benny turned to see a silver-haired gentleman seated at a table near them. "I'm a reporter for the *Smith Falls Times*," the silver-haired man said, pressing the button on the side of a tiny tape recorder. "I would love to ask you a few questions for the paper."

"Of course!" said Fran, stepping forward with a smile. "You should see the white dresses! They're kind of flouncy and go all the way down to the floor. They're so pretty!"

"Did it take a long time to make all the white Kleenex flowers?" asked the newspaper reporter, holding up the tape recorder for Fran to talk into.

Benny noticed how slowly the tiny spool in the tape recorder turned. He noticed how easily Fran answered his questions. Benny noticed something else, too. He noticed the black silhouette of a teenaged boy who looked like JP edging up behind Rosie.

JP tapped the arm of a passing waiter and nodded his curly head in their direction. "Get a load of these scaredy-cat detectives," JP laughed.

Benny stiffened. *Scaredy-cat detectives?* Benny turned to face JP. Benny's ears rose alertly on his head. The hair down his spine bristled. *Who, exactly, was JP calling scaredy-cat detectives?*

JP crept up carefully behind Rosie, then pounced to land right in front of her. "BOO!" he yelled. He looked at Rosie through his dark black curls and waggled his fingers spookily in the air. "Did I scare you? Ha-ha-ha-ha!"

Benny didn't wait for Rosie's reply. He had already jerked his leash free from Rosie's hand and was chasing JP across the stage, around the drums (WHAM! BAM! CLANK!), and between the candlelit tables.

"Don't!" JP yelled as he ran. "Don't bite!"

"Benny!" called someone who sounded a lot like Rosie. "Benny, come back! Ben-*ny! NOW!*"

"*RRRRRRR!*" Benny growled as he ran.

"JP!" laughed some young men who were sitting around a table of drinks at a corner table. "Run faster!"

"*Don't* run JP!" yelled someone else. "You're making it worse!"

"Play dead!" the young men called out, laughing and thumping the table.

"No, stupid! That's for bears!"

"*RRRRRRRRRR!*" Benny was still growling as he tried to clamp his teeth on the bottom of JP's black T-shirt. *Scaredy-cat detectives?* Benny fumed. *I don't believe I'm acquainted with any scaredy-cat detectives!*

"BENNY! COME HERE!" Benny heard someone that sounded like Mr. Bensky shouting. "COME HERE NOW! BAD DOG!"

But by then, Benny was pursuing JP through the kitchen (so many feet! so many pots! so many smells!) and out into the hallway. He leapt over a metal beer keg lying on its side.

Suddenly a large muscular arm opened a fire door, blocking Benny's way, and a hard foot booted Benny outside.

"NO DOGS ALLOWED! GOT THAT?" yelled a large aproned man. Then the door slammed on Benny.

Benny stood on a metal fire escape, his leash still dangling around his neck. He blinked his eyes rapidly, still breathless from the chase.

Gosh! What just happened? Benny asked himself. *Where am I?*

Cautiously, while his eyes gradually adapted to the darkness, Benny made his way down the fire escape.

The back alley had a row of garbage cans along one side, a broken chair, a bicycle chained to a post, and a white van with lettering on the side.

"All alone? No owner?" said a man who sat behind the steering wheel of the van. The man looked up the darkened alley in both directions, then climbed out. "Come along then, buddy," he said, bending down to take Benny's collar. The man spoke in such an authoritative way that Benny didn't think to question him. He allowed the man to lead him to the back of the white van, then – with a little help from the man – Benny stepped up into the back of the vehicle.

"Good boy," the man said encouragingly. The man shut a cage door, then another outer door.

But when the man got behind the wheel and began to drive, Benny's doggie brain connected. *This is not right!* Benny thought. *It is not right to be in the back of a moving van without Rosie or Fran or Mr. or Mrs. Bensky!*

"RUFF! RUFF! RUFF!" Benny protested. "BOW-WOW-WOW! RUFF! RUFF! RUFF!"

But the man, who sat on the other side of a metal grid, only glanced back at him through the rearview mirror. Before long, the man stopped the van, opened the back door, and led Benny up the wide concrete steps of a large building. A lit up sign with many letters spelled out some words, S-M-I-T-H F-A-L-L-S A-N-I-M-A-L S-H-E-L-T-E-R. But without Rosie and Fran to coach him, Benny couldn't guess what the letters meant.

Inside the brightly lit building, the man passed a desk where he called out, "Sixty-five-pound male canine, black with brown eyebrows, mixed breed." The gum-chewing woman behind the desk seemed to write that down.

Benny turned his head and tried to pull his way back to the door. But the burly man had a firm hold on his collar.

"No worries, buddy," the man said in the same in-charge voice.

But this time Benny didn't believe him. Benny Bensky braced his feet against the concrete floor, trying desperately to shake his head free from the man's grip. He growled and snapped and lunged with all his strength toward the door. But the man held him firmly. Two other men appeared from a back room and clamped a muzzle around Benny's mouth. One man pulled on his leash while the other man pushed at his rump, forcing Benny in the opposite direction, farther into the building.

They pulled him through a hallway, then into a brightly lit room that was thunderous with barking.

"Help! Help!" the dogs barked from cages on all sides.

"Let me out of here!" barked a tiny dog with huge ears.

"I want my mum!" cried another wiry spotted dog.

"Come here and I'll bite your ugly head off!" a huge rust-colored dog snarled, lunging toward Benny, but smacking hard against the metal bars of his cage.

The air smelled of doggie pee. It smelled of doggie poo.

The men opened a metal cage, shoved Benny in, then slammed the door – *CLANK!* – behind him. Benny lay alone, his paws covering his eyes as best he could. He was cold, lost, and trembling. *Rosie? Fran?* he asked himself.

But Rosie and Fran weren't there!

They aren't here! THEY AREN'T HERE!

Benny's heart thumped in his throat. He felt as though he was falling into a deep, deep, deep, deep black hole.

Benny had been lying in his cold dark cage for what seemed like a long time, afraid to move, when he heard something that made him lift one paw from one eye. He pricked up one ear. He pricked up both ears!

"One hundred dollars!" he heard a familiar voice yelling.

Benny leapt to his feet and looked out of a tiny crack in the door of his cage. Benny saw a light shining off a bald head. Why, it looked like Mr. Bensky's bald head! Benny leapt about and whimpered.

"That dog's only worth .829 of a cent," the bald-headed man insisted. "It's a proven fact! Get me a calculator and I'll prove it to you!"

"The standard fine is one hundred dollars, Sir," the gum-chewing woman explained. "Regardless of what breed your dog is. It would have been two hundred dollars if we'd picked him up without a leash."

"See, the leash shows we were trying, Daddy," another voice said. Rosie's voice!

Let me out! Benny yelped joyously, "YIPE! YIPE! YIPE!" *Let me out!*

Suddenly, the cage door opened and Benny exploded into Rosie's and Fran's arms. He peed joyously into the air. Rosie and Fran laughed and hugged him. But when Benny leapt up to kiss Mr. Bensky's face, Mr. Bensky only stared down at Benny, his face red and scowly, his hairy arms crossed in front of him.

"Into the car," growled Mr. Bensky. "It's late and I'm tired. We're going straight home to bed. And not *a single word* from any one of you!"

Benny sat in the dark backseat between Rosie and Fran. The lights from the street reflected off their toothy smiles. Mr. Bensky hunched over the wheel. Benny grinned so widely it felt like he might turn inside out. His black nose shone. His heart drummed inside his chest. *Mr. Bensky just paid one hundred dollars to get me out,* Benny told himself. *That proves that I'm worth more than one cent. Doesn't it?*

Benny reached forward and quickly placed a big slurpy kiss on the back of Mr. Bensky's sweaty neck.

Just Leave Me Alone!

Benny Bensky was dreaming about chasing Frisbees that kept changing into parrots, when he woke to banging on the front door.

Benny bumped up against Rosie with his black nose. He smelled the bed sheets. He licked his own paw. *It's true! It's not just a dream! I really am home!* Benny leapt high into the air and kissed Rosie for the hundredth time.

"Okay, Fran," mumbled Rosie. She rubbed her eyes and made her way down the stairs with Benny.

(No one but Fran ever knocked on their door this early in the morning.)

"I saw something!" said Fran when they opened the door. "Come on, guys! I just saw a gray bird on top of Mr. Gormley's house!"

"A gray bird? Was it Peanut?" asked Rosie. "You saw Peanut?"

"Come on!" said Fran.

Barefoot and still in her flamingo-patterned pajamas, Rosie and Benny ran after Fran, toward Mr. Gormley's house farther down the street.

"*Pea*-nut!" called the girls as they ran. "*Pea*-nut!"

By the time Benny got to Mr. Gormley's house, Fran had hopped onto the neighbor's fence, into an apple tree, and was now scrambling up the porch roof.

"Peanut?" called Fran.

Benny heard a scratching, scrambling sound, almost exactly like the sound Peanut made when he was locked in the garbage can! Benny whimpered with excitement.

"Come out, come out, wherever you are!" called Rosie from the ground.

There was more rustling and scratching, then suddenly – movement! Pigeons exploded from the eaves.

The air was filled with the sound of moving wings. Fran threw up her arms and shrieked, and Benny, on the lawn below, barked furiously.

"Pigeons!" said Fran from the roof. "They were only pigeons!"

"Are you sure?" said Rosie from the front lawn. "Wasn't even *one* of those birds a parrot?"

"What does a fellow have to do to get a little sleep around here?" said Mr. Gormley, sticking his head out of the second-floor window. "Oh, no! Don't tell me! I suppose you think *I'm* the parrot-napper."

"Are you?" asked Rosie hopefully from the ground below.

"No, I am *not*! Now go home, do your detective work in your own yard and leave me in peace!" Mr. Gormley slammed his window shut.

"Girls! Girls!" said Mrs. Bensky, running toward them and calling out in a hushed voice. She looked sleepy and was holding her bathrobe shut with one hand. "It's not even 6 a.m.! Let our poor neighbors sleep!"

"At least Mr. Gormley's off our suspect list," said Fran, still slightly embarrassed to have been scolded by Mr. Gormley.

"Yes, he is," agreed Rosie.

Benny walked alongside of his friends, glad that Rosie had been kind enough not to point out that Mr. Gormley had never been *on* the suspect list in the first place.

"Swear by this sword!" Mr. Bensky was shouting dramatically when they got back into the house. Mr.

Bensky was dressed in his tights and fencing with the kitchen whisk in front of the mirror. "Tell me girls," he said, turning to them. "Do I look more distinguished with or without this mustache?" He pulled a fake handlebar mustache from his shirt pocket and stuck it on top of his own short bristly mustache. "With or without?"

"With, Mr. Bensky," said Fran.

"Yes, with, Daddy," said Rosie.

"Good gracious!" said Mrs. Bensky, who was bringing in the morning paper. "Fran! Your picture is on the front page of the *Smith Falls Times*!"

Everyone, Benny included, crowded around the newspaper and peered down at it.

"Young Actor Plays Flower Girl," the headline read. And right beneath was a large picture of Fran, a wide happy smile on her face. Behind Fran, you could see a shirt button – possibly Mr. Bensky's – also someone's ear – possibly Rosie's.

Mrs. Bensky read the article aloud: "Fran Lee, a ten-year-old resident of Smith Falls, is looking forward to playing the flower girl in *Hamlet*, which is one of the plays in this year's theater festival. Ms. Lee says she is looking forward to wearing the white dress, which is her costume for the flower-girl role.

'I'm so excited,' Ms. Fran Lee told the *Smith Falls Times*. 'I am going to be the best flower girl ever! I made the flowers myself. I'm good with my hands, so it didn't take me very long. I will be wearing a very beautiful white dress. I'm really looking forward to throwing the flowers. I feel like I was born to do this. I know my mother will be very proud!'"

"That's funny," said Rosie, when her mother had finished reading. She pushed up her glasses and looked at Fran. "It's all about *you*. It sounds like there's only *one* flower girl."

"I'm sure I mentioned you, too," said Fran, her cheeks very pink.

"It doesn't sound like it," said Rosie.

"You didn't even *want* to be in the play, Rosie!" accused Fran.

"But I *am* in it!"

"Girls, girls," said Mrs. Bensky. "Sometimes good friends have disagreements. But you have to talk about what's bothering you."

"What's bothering me is Fran thinking just about herself," said Rosie, folding her arms across her chest. Her face was stormy.

"I'm *not* just thinking about myself, Rosie!" Fran insisted. "I'm the one who's thinking about Peanut!

We have to find Peanut *today*! Because tonight is the play and tomorrow morning Mrs. Graham will be back! We have to go check out JP again, Rosie!"

"Oh, no you don't!" said Mr. Bensky loudly and firmly. "You kids leave JP alone! Enough is enough!"

"Why did he scream and run anyway?" said Fran. "Everyone knows you shouldn't scream and run when a dog is after you!"

"Benny was trying to protect me," said Rosie. "At least I have *one* friend!"

Benny looked unhappily from Rosie to Fran and Fran to Rosie, but he didn't know what to do. Rosie and Fran had never had a quarrel like this before. Sometimes they argued about who should hold the popcorn when they watched a video, but they usually solved that by (very sensibly!) placing the bowl in front of Benny.

"I *am* your friend, Rosie! I *am*! Remember the Detective Squad?"

Yes! We're a team! Benny ran from one girl to the other, nudging Rosie first, then Fran and running around them as if tangling them together with invisible string.

"Just leave me alone, Fran!" Rosie shouted, tears sliding down her cheeks. "I don't want to be your friend anymore!"

10

The Play's the Thing!

*T**his play,* thought Benny, *is taking an awfully long time to get finished.* There had been a lot of speeches, soldiers with swords, and even a ghost (a very boring, long-winded ghost, in Benny's opinion).

Every once in a while, Rosie and Fran, both in white dresses and on opposite wings of the stage, pelted each other with white Kleenex flowers.

"To be or not to be," a mustached Mr. Bensky was pronouncing from the spotlight on stage. "That, indeed, is the question."

Whap! Whap! Two flowers flew from stage left,

where Rosie was situated, to stage right, where Fran was standing.

Whap! Whap! Two white Kleenex flowers flew straight back from stage right and hit Rosie.

"Ouch!" Rosie said aloud. Hamlet (that is, Mr. Bensky) put his hands on his hips, cleared his throat, and glared, first at Rosie, then at Fran.

Mr. Gormley, in the second row, snored lightly. Police Officers Sue and Sam fanned their faces with their police officer caps. JP, in his torn skull-and-crossbones T-shirt, openly twiddled his thumbs. Mr. Bellefleur sat regally at the front, following the script that he held in his hands. His red cape was thrown over his shoulders, his purple beret perched aslant on his head.

It was a hot summer night and the fire doors of the auditorium were held wide open by bricks, but not a single whisper of a breeze reached Benny.

Benny stood up, jingling his tags and thumping about as he tried to find a more comfortable position on the hard wooden floor of the community center.

A finely dressed lady ahead of him turned around and looked down at Benny. "Would you please stop panting?" she said. "It's interfering with my concentration."

Benny ducked his head in embarrassment, accidentally jangling his tags again. He tiptoed to the open door, his toenails clicking on the wooden floor. The finely dressed lady frowned in his direction.

Benny stepped just outside the door. *Ahhh! It's so much fresher out here!* Benny held his head high in the delicately scented breeze. From the open doorway he could smell cut grass, lawnmower fumes, and the metallic garbage-y smell of the garbage can!

He crept out a bit farther. *I'll bet it's even nicer over here,* Benny told himself as he walked to the bricked-in area at the front of the community center. From inside the building, there was the sound of a bugle and another speech.

Benny trailed farther down the walk, then a bit farther again, scouting about for a piece of bagel, a slice of bologna, or some interesting cat smells. *Hmmmm.* Benny looked up. A white van! A white van was approaching!

Benny dived into the nearest gate – Mr. Bellefleur's gate – and ran down the walk to the back. But Mr. Bellefleur's backyard was a flat square lawn without a single bush or shrub to hide behind! Benny ran up the back steps and into the tiny back porch. What to do? Benny turned around, hoping to crouch down low and hide his face in his paws to look like some other sleeping dog (not the sixty-five-pound, black-with-brown-eyebrows, mixed-breed dog the shelter already had a file on). But Benny's ample rump thumped against the back door and it creaked open.

What was this? A moldy smell? A feathery, musty, parrot-y smell? *Where, exactly,* Benny asked himself, *is that smell coming from?*

Benny stepped very stealthily into the kitchen, where the parrot-y smell was even stronger. He raised his rubbery black nose high in the air and sniffed about with increasing excitement.

But there were no parrots anywhere! Benny checked in front of the fridge, on top of the garbage can, and inside the garbage can. He went to the front room and looked up high on the curtain rod. Where else could a parrot be found?

Then Benny looked down at the coffee table. There was one feather – dowdy, dull, gray, parrot-y-smelling – undoubtedly Peanut's!

"RUFF! RUFF!" Benny barked excitedly. "RUFF! RUFF!" He jumped up on the couch and it creaked.

"Bad boy, Benny!" someone called out. Benny's head whirled about.

"Bad boy, Benny! Off the couch, Benny!" the voice shouted again. Why, it was Peanut's voice!

At that moment, the door of an antique closet fell open. Instantly, the air was full of squawking parrots! Green parrots, red parrots, blue parrots, ruffled parrots, smooth parrots! Somewhere in that dark whirling cloud, Benny thought he caught a glimpse of a dowdy gray parrot that looked like Peanut.

All of the parrots were screeching loudly, swooping back and forth across the room, then diving down at Benny. Their beaks pinched like clothespins!

YIPES! Benny yelped, jumping down from the couch to the floor. The parrots were nipping his ears! They were nipping his nose! Benny ran into the kitchen and out into the backyard, but the swarm of shrieking, nipping parrots flew right after him.

Benny braced himself on all fours and shook them off for a moment, but, like a swarm of gigantic mosquitoes, they immediately descended upon him again. He tried rolling on the grass, but then the parrots bit his toes. *YIPES! Double YIPES!*

Benny had a plan. Not a well-considered plan, it was true – who had time for a well-considered plan with this swarm of crazy parrots nipping and clawing at them?

Benny ran as quickly as he could go, the cloud of noisy parrots close behind: out Mr. Bellefleur's gate, past Mrs. Graham's house, and back to the community center where – with a great noisy *WHOOSH!* – the parrots followed Benny through the open fire door and down the center aisle toward the stage.

Mr. Bensky was in the spotlight, wearing his black tights and holding a plastic skull in his hand. "Alas, poor Yorick," he was saying. Then he looked up, startled to see the dark cloud of parrots closing in on him.

"Help! Get away from me! Stop pecking! Help! NO!" Mr. Bensky yelled as the parrots attacked him. Mr. Bensky swished his plastic sword at the nipping parrots and ran to one end of the stage, then the other. White Kleenex flowers flew like snowballs. "Hey! That's my mustache! That's not funny! Give it back!"

"Hands up you parrot-napping varmint!" yelled Peanut loudly, from the top of Mr. Bensky's bald head. "Yesh! I mean you!"

Instantly, the auditorium became silent. Peanut's words seemed to echo in the hall. Everybody looked around at their neighbors.

Slowly, Mr. Bellefleur's hands went up. "What are you doing, you crazy parrots?" he shouted. "Why

are you here *now*? You're not in *Hamlet*! You're in
The Birds, you idiots! You're supposed to attack in
The Birds!"

Police Officer Sam stood up and placed his cap on
his head. "For the time being, these parrots are not

involved in any play at all," he said quietly. "And neither, I'm afraid, are you." He slipped a pair of handcuffs on Mr. Bellefleur's wrists. "Mr. Bellefleur, I hereby arrest you for the unlawful parrot-napping of the parrots of Smith Falls. You have the right to remain silent. What you say can and will be held against you in a court of law."

"Those stupid parrots!" raged Mr. Bellefleur, as he was led away. "If they would only follow my direction, none of this would have happened!"

"Elmer! Mavis!" Mr. Bittle called, jumping up to retrieve his parrots. "You're back!"

"Nipper! Napper! Noo-Noo! Natch!" called Mrs. Russo joyously. "Nelly! Norma! Noodle!" Grinning, JP got up and stretched out his lanky arms to help her with the parrots.

Rosie and Fran and Benny didn't have to call Peanut, for Peanut the Parrot was already sitting on Fran's shoulder and tugging a shiny barrette out of her hair.

"Oh, Peanut!" laughed Rosie, "I'm *so* glad to see you!"

Rosie turned to Fran and Fran turned to Rosie. The girls looked at each other.

"I'm really sorry I hurt your feelings, Rosie," said Fran quietly.

"I'm okay now," answered Rosie.

The girls hugged hard, so hard they groaned. Then they laughed. While they were still in each other's arms, Peanut climbed from Fran's shoulder to Rosie's shoulder.

"Hands up you parrot-napping varmint! Yesh! I mean you!" yelled Peanut.

Around them, everyone was happily discussing the play. "So original!" the finely dressed lady was saying. "So interactive!"

"Great effects!" exclaimed someone else.

"A real tearjerker!"

Personally, grinned Benny, *I loved the ending!*

What a Dog! What a Detective!

Early next morning, while the SORRY, WE'RE CLOSED sign was still up, there was a tap on the Perogy Palace window.

The Bensky family and Fran looked up to see Police Officers Sam and Sue waving cheerily from outside the restaurant.

"We've come for a cup of that top-notch Perogy House coffee!" Police Officer Sue said when Mr. Bensky opened the door.

"No, you haven't!" said Mr. Bensky with mock gruffness. Then he grinned and added, "You've come for a big plate of perogies, too! Sit down with us! Here! Here! At this big round table near the kitchen door. The tourists are coming to town for the theater festival, and I'm a happy man again!"

"Our favorite table!" laughed Police Officer Sam.

"Ours too!" squeaked Billy Bittle, who popped his head inside the door.

"Friends! Welcome!" boomed Mr. Bensky, pulling out chairs at the table for Mr. and Mrs. Bittle.

"I can't tell you how happy we are, dearies!" said Mrs. Bittle settling her stout self next to Rosie and Fran and Benny. "Billy just adores his parrots, yes indeedy! We've come to tell you how grateful we are."

"Benny did most of it," said Rosie, and Benny grinned up at his friends.

"If it wasn't for Benny and his amazing detective know-how, my birds would still be sitting in a dark closet in Mr. Bellefleur's house!" said Billy Bittle in his squeaky voice.

"Like I was explaining," said Police Officer Sam. "A dog has two billion olfactory receptor cells to smell with, while humans have only forty million."

"Two billion versus a puny forty million. Hey! No fair!" complained Mr. Bensky in his humorous way.

"Benny can smell a tennis ball even if it's caught underneath all the cushions on the couch," explained Rosie eagerly.

"He can smell a jelly bean underneath the carpet!" said Fran proudly.

"That dog's real smart," said Mr. Bensky.

"What a dog!" said Police Officer Sue.

"What a darned good detective!" said Police Officer Sam.

Benny grinned modestly. His tail banged musically against a stainless-steel cart. *Tring-tring! Tring-tring!*

"We helped, too!" said Rosie quickly.

"We did!" said Fran. "I saw the wing in Mr. Bellefleur's window, remember?" Then she looked at Rosie. "But, I couldn't have solved the mystery on my own. We did it together! We were a team!"

Benny grinned and tring-tringed his tail against the cart again. *An amazing team,* he agreed. *All in all, an incredible and amazing team.*

"Peanut, too!" said Fran.

"Yes, Peanut helped," said Rosie.

The Perogy Palace door opened again and everyone turned to look.

Mrs. Graham, holding a large flowered handbag in one hand and Peanut in a carrying cage in the other, walked boldly through the door of the restaurant with its SORRY, WE'RE CLOSED sign. Mrs. Graham had a huge smile on her face.

"I hoped I could find you here," she beamed. "First of all, I want to thank Rosie and Fran and Benny for the wonderful job they did baby-sitting my dear Peanut."

"Hands up you parrot-napping varmint! Yesh! I mean you!" yelled Peanut.

"He just loves saying that!" laughed Mrs. Graham. "I can't imagine why! Now, I've brought you girls brand-new, parrot-patterned T-shirts as a souvenir."

"Thank you!" said Rosie and Fran happily. They pulled on their new parrot-patterned T-shirts right over the ones they were already wearing.

"Now, everyone. Stay right where you are," continued Mrs. Graham. "I've brought a few snapshots of the triplets."

"Triplets?" laughed Mrs. Bensky. She hugged Mrs. Graham. "Did you say *triplets*?"

"I'm so excited," said Mrs. Graham, putting Peanut's cage down beside a dish of perogies. "Shall I pass the photos around clockwise? Now, this is Millie and this is Tillie and this is Willie. Or is *this* Tillie?"

"Mummy! Mummy!" said Rosie. "Can we get triplets, too? *Pleeeeease* mummy?"

"Fran! Rosie! Listen girls," said Mrs. Graham in her commanding way. "You must promise to baby-sit. Please, please, *please* don't say no! You see, Anna is coming to visit at the end of the month with Willie and Tillie and Millie and we're going to need plenty of help."

"Goody-goody gumdrops!" yelled Fran and Rosie together, clapping their hands.

Oh, no, thought Benny, dropping his head between his paws and covering his eyes. *Not again!*

Rosie held a snapshot of the triplets down for Benny to see. Benny just stared. *Three of them this time!*

Rosie bent down and hugged Benny's furry head. "Don't worry, Benny," she whispered, reading his thoughts, just as she used to. "They can't talk."

"They can't walk either," said Fran.

"Or fly," laughed Mr. Bensky. "Let's hope not anyway."

"Talk? Walk? Good gracious, no!" exclaimed Mrs. Graham. "Not for a year or more! Why, I remember Anna's first word! She said 'Ma-ma!' Just like that! Clear as a little bell!"

"Rosie's first word was 'Da-da!'" Mr. Bensky grinned proudly. "I was feeding her cream of wheat one day – brown sugar and cream, like always – and she looked straight into my eyes and said, 'Da-da!'"

"Da-da!" Peanut screeched and everyone laughed.

"It's all in the nose!" Police Officer Sue was explaining to Mrs. Bittle. "Dogs have a truly superior sense of smell!"

"Now, look at *this* nose," Mrs. Graham said to Mrs. Bensky. "See how it goes down in a single straight line? That's a Graham nose. And those ears? Those are Graham ears!"

Police Officer Sue's cell phone beeped.

"Police Officer Sue," she said quietly. She listened for a moment before she spoke. "We'll be right there. New investigation," she explained to the table as she and Police Officer Sam rose to their feet. "Benny, Rosie, Fran, we'll call you if we need help."

"Thanks for the assistance, Benny," Police Officer Sam said quietly, shaking Benny's paw.

Benny lifted his paw and shook again.

"What a dog! What a detective!" said Police Officer Sue, bending down to give Benny a hug and shaking his paw several more times.

"What a dog! What a detective!" echoed Peanut in his screechy voice. He flipped around on his perch and flapped his wings.

Benny, who had settled down at Rosie's feet, looked up at Peanut. He remembered the pale-green couch. He remembered the shredded phone book. He remembered the scrabbling sound Peanut made when he was locked inside the garbage can. He remembered seeing Peanut's dowdy gray feather on

Mr. Bellefleur's coffee table. He remembered the clothespin pecks of the screeching parrots. He remembered Peanut flying across the auditorium and landing on Fran's shoulder. He remembered Rosie and Fran hugging each other and making up.

"What a dog! What a detective!" Peanut squawked, bobbing on his perch inside the cage. "What a dog! What a detective!"

I guess that bird IS sort of cute, Benny said to himself, sitting up to look at Peanut. Benny tilted his head one way and then the other. *Maybe a little.* Then Benny grinned broadly. *For a birdbrain.*

Benny Bensky's Big-Bite Doggie Biscuits

Place the following ingredients into a mixing bowl:

1½ cups whole wheat flour
½ cup grated cheese
¼ cup bacon fat (or softened butter)
½ cup water
1 tablespoon soy sauce
1 to 2 tablespoons chopped parsley (optional)

Mix. Shape – a little extra flour may be needed. Place on a greased sheet. Bake until golden brown (18 to 20 minutes) at 400 degrees Fahrenheit.

Your dog will love these biscuits!

Also available by Mary Borsky

Benny Bensky and the Perogy Palace
Benny Bensky used to be a happy dog living with his human family, the Benskys. But things are not happy in the Bensky household: The family's restaurant, the Perogy Palace, used to be the most popular place to eat in town, but now, people are staying away in droves.

What's worse, Benny's family is fed up with his bad habits, and they are sending him to obedience school! Benny, terrified of the persnickety instructor, fails the class miserably. But while he's there, Benny sniffs out the problem behind the Perogy Palace's loss of customers. What's a dog with imagination to do?

Benny Bensky and the Giant Pumpkin Heist
Benny Bensky is a big black dog with a nose for trouble. His owner, Rosie, and her best friend, Fran, are growing a giant pumpkin for the Giant Pumpkin Weigh-Off, and it looks like the first prize is within their reach. But soon, Benny and the girls are involved in solving a nefarious crime: someone is stealing the pumpkins and, even worse, the detective trio is getting the blame!

About the Author

Mary Borsky is originally from High Prairie in northern Alberta. She received her bachelor's degree from the University of Alberta and went on to teach. Borsky is the author of the first two books in the Benny Bensky series, *Benny Bensky and the Perogy Palace* and *Benny Bensky and the Giant Pumpkin Heist*. In 2006, *The New Quarterly* magazine named Mary Borsky one of the "best-loved living Canadian writers." Mary Borsky lives in Ottawa with her family.